Football School
Name:.......................................
Class:....................................
Coaches:.........................
KICKITO ERGO SUM

For ABC, with love – B. L.

First published 2025 by Walker Books Ltd
87 Vauxhall Walk, London SE11 5HJ

2 4 6 8 10 9 7 5 3 1

EU Authorized Representative: HackettFlynn Ltd, 36 Cloch Choirneal, Balrothery, Co. Dublin, K32 C942, Ireland. EU@walkerpublishinggroup.com

This book has been typeset in Gill Sans MT Pro and WB-ART Spike

Printed in China

British Library Cataloguing in Publication Data:
a catalogue record for this book is available from the British Library

ISBN 978-1-5295-2600-4

www.walker.co.uk
footballschool.co

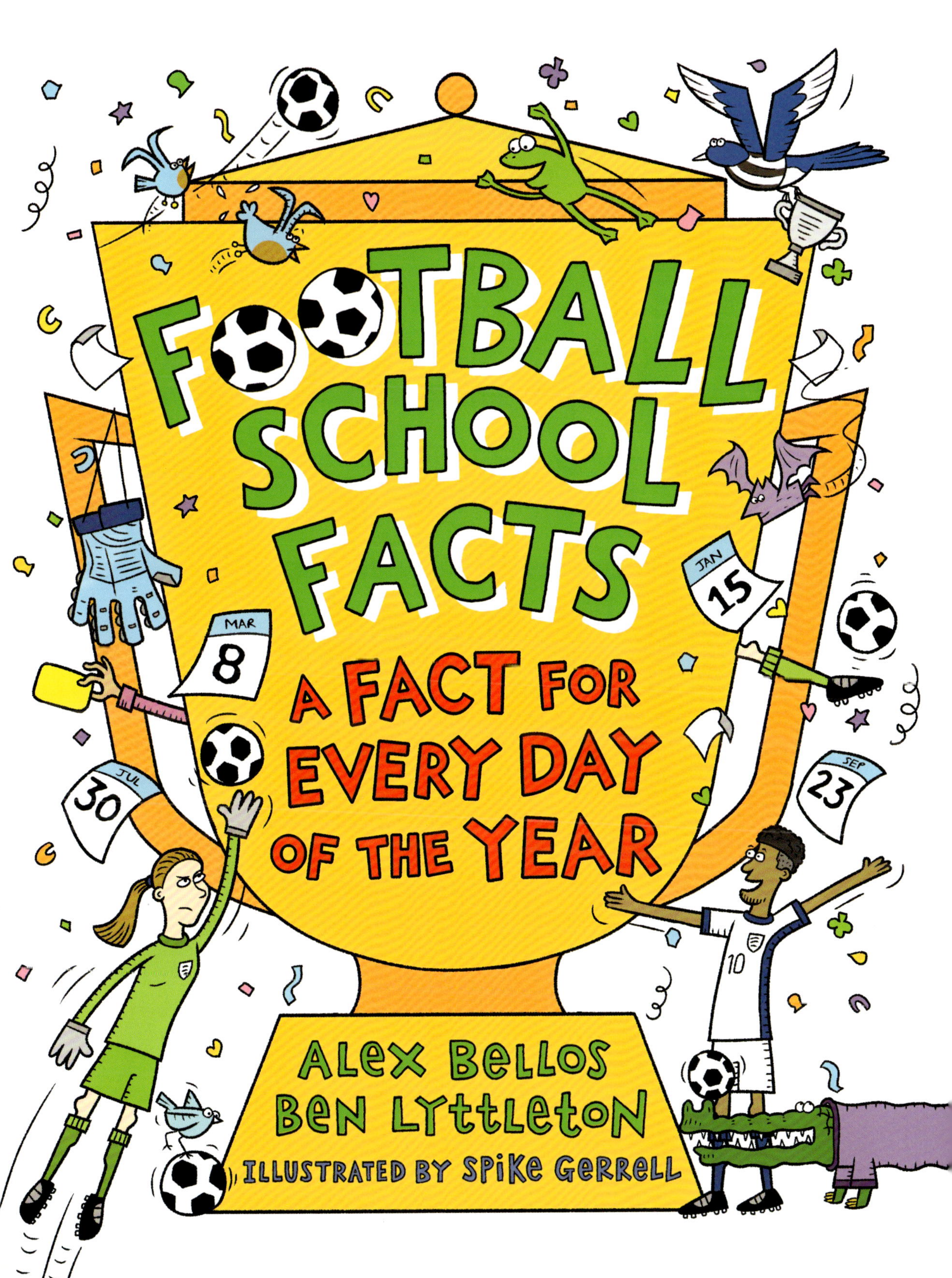

FOOTBALL SCHOOL FACTS
A FACT FOR EVERY DAY OF THE YEAR
ALEX BELLOS
BEN LYTTLETON
ILLUSTRATED BY SPIKE GERRELL
MAR
8
JAN
15
JUL
30
SEP
23
10

-CONTENTS-

-INTRODUCTION-

Welcome to *Football School Facts: A Fact for Every Day of the Year*. Let's start by getting our facts straight: if you love football, you will love this book. We've written about the game in all its forms: from players, pitches and penalties, through referees, red cards and record-breakers to tournaments, trophies and tricks.

There's something for all the family: twins who have played for their national teams and a brother-and-sister duo who have both played for England. To mix it up, there's the goalkeeper who does magic tricks on the pitch and a player who was sent off for farting. Not to be sniffed at! We'll even travel to the country whose league season lasts just one week and to another with a league for players aged over 80. Old school!

A football match lasts 90 minutes and is divided into two halves. This book lasts for 366 days (well, it could do) and is divided into twelve chapters – one for each month. We kick off every chapter with a gallery of players who celebrate their birthdays that month. In most cases, there's a team of eleven players who would make a good starting line-up if they all played together (even if one or two are very old or, in a few cases, sadly no longer with us). See if you can work out which position each of these players would play in – and, of course, if a birthday matches your own!

Some of our facts focus on an individual whose birthday falls on that day. When that happens, keep an eye out for the birthday icon, shown here: We've even included the birthday icons for Alex and Ben, so you can see when we were born (quite a long time ago!).

You will also see an icon that looks like this: Can you guess what that means? Very good! It means that this fact happened on the *exact* day that you are reading about. It's a moment in history that will never be forgotten. At least, not now!

Look out, too, for the themed double pages in each month, often with a seasonal twist, and for the mind-twisting quiz that appears, in true *Football School* style, at the end of each chapter. And to celebrate Christmas and the end of the year, we've created an extra-special double page of puzzles to see if you've remembered the facts from the book.

We learned so many facts about football and the world as we wrote this book, and we are excited to share them all with you. As a matter of fact, we're sure you will love them. Fact check complete: it's time to get started. Enjoy!

Alex and Ben

Year we go, year we go,
year we go!
FOOTBALL
SCHOOL

JANUARY

JANUARY BIRTHDAYS

LUIS DÍAZ

JAN 13

Colombian winger, joint-top scorer in the 2021 Copa América

DECLAN RICE

JAN 14

England midfielder, brilliant ball-winner who can start attacks

AITANA BONMATÍ

JAN 18

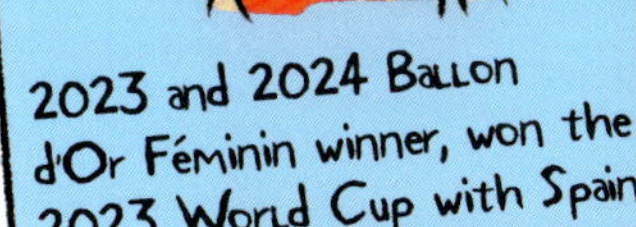

2023 and 2024 Ballon d'Or Féminin winner, won the 2023 World Cup with Spain

PEP GUARDIOLA

JAN 18

Former Barcelona player, now one of the most influential coaches of the modern era

JOŠKO GVARDIOL

JAN 23

Croatian defender, one of the best in the world, Manchester City title winner

EUSÉBIO

JAN 25

Portuguese 1965 Ballon d'Or winner and top scorer at the 1966 World Cup

GIGI BUFFON

JAN 28

Played a record 176 times for Italy, winning the 2006 World Cup

JAN 1

STILL SCORING, SIR!

In the New Year's Day honours list of 1965, Stanley Matthews became the first British player to be awarded a knighthood, the title of Sir, while still a player. Matthews was nineteen when he scored his first England goal in 1934 – and 41 when he scored his last. His goalscoring run lasted 22 years and seven days. This has since been bettered by USA forward Kristine Lilly, who scored her first international goal aged sixteen in 1986 and her final goal, number 130, when she was 38 – an amazing 22 years and 282 days later.

JAN 2

SPEECHLESS

Don't be cross if you see Spain players not singing their national anthem before an international match. Their anthem, *La Marcha Real*, does not have any words! The only other countries with no words in their national anthems are Bosnia and Herzegovina, San Marino and Kosovo.

JAN 3

ON THE MOVE

A football transfer is when a player moves from one club to another. The transfers that make the biggest headlines are the ones involving the most money – but most transfers, about two-thirds of them, take place when players come to the end of their contracts and move for nothing.

JAN 4

DEEP FREEZE

The 1963 Scottish Cup tie between Airdrie and Stranraer was postponed 33 times after freezing conditions meant the whole season had to be extended by one month. When the game was finally played, Airdrie won 3–0 – but then lost 6–0 to Rangers in the next round!

JAN 5

FOGGY FIFTEEN

During a winter fixture in 1937 between Chelsea and Charlton, the fog in London was so bad that the match was abandoned after one hour, but no one told the Charlton goalkeeper, Sam Bartram. He stayed on the pitch for an extra fifteen minutes, thinking the game was still taking place. He was found by a policeman, who directed him to the dressing room. His team-mates were all showered and ready to go home.

JAN 6

ON THE SLIDE

South Korean side Gangwon play their matches at the Alpensia Ski Jump Stadium. It has a giant ski slope behind one of the goals, built to host the 2018 Winter Olympics. During winter, the pitch is where the ski-jumpers land; in summer, the pitch is used for football. That's one way to get a jump on the opposition!

JAN 7

THINK PINK

Pink shirts are not common in football. Yet the biggest club in Italy, Juventus, wore pink when they were first formed in 1897. They changed to their famous black-and-white vertical stripes in 1903, copying English side Notts County, who were then a well-known team. Juventus still use pink shirts for away games. Other teams that wear pink for home matches now are Evian (France), Palermo (Italy), Cerezo Osaka (Japan) and Inter Miami (USA).

JAN 8

A LONG WAY FROM HOME

France governs islands a long way from Europe, such as Réunion in the Indian Ocean and New Caledonia in the Pacific. Teams from these places sometimes play in the Coupe de France, the French equivalent of the FA Cup, flying across the world to compete. Amateur side JS Saint-Pierroise, from Réunion, did just that in 2020: they travelled over 9,600 kilometres and beat French Ligue 2 side Niort, only to lose 1–0 in extra-time in the next round. So near and yet so very, very far!

JAN 9

MASCOT RED-CARDED

Reading had their giant lion mascot, Kingsley Royal, sent off during a match in 2014. He was standing on the side of the pitch wearing a Reading kit, which confused the referee.

JAN 10

FULL TO THE RIMET

The first World Cup, held in Uruguay in 1930, was the idea of Jules Rimet, a football-loving Frenchman who wanted to organize a football tournament to bring nations together. Thirteen countries took part in the 1930 tournament. At the 2026 World Cup, over 200 nations will attempt to qualify for the tournament, with 48 teams making it.

Year of the World Cup	Number of teams
1930	13
1934–38	16
1950	13
1954–78	16
1982–94	24
1998–2022	32
2026	48

JAN 11

BRONZE RECORDS

Lucy Bronze is the first English female player to win the Women's Champions League with two different clubs: three times at Lyon and once with Barcelona. The full-back, who helped England win Euro 2022, could have played for Scotland, as she has Scottish relatives, or Portugal, as her dad was born there.

JAN 12

NO LOOPS IN HULL

Hull City is the only team in the top four English leagues with a name that you can't colour in. What we mean is that it is the only team that does not contain any of the letters a, b, d, e, g, o, p, q, which are the letters that include closed loops that you can colour in.

JAN 13

YOU CAN DO IT

In World Cup penalty shoot-outs, the rate of scoring when that penalty will win the shoot-out is 92 per cent. That rate drops to 62 per cent when the kick is to avoid defeat in the shoot-out. This shows the power of thinking about positive rather than negative consequences.

JAN 14

RICE CAKES

Declan Rice gets his energy for non-stop running around the pitch from a diet of pancakes before matches. The England midfielder eats four pancakes with honey before every game and claims it boosts his energy.

JAN 15

NORTH GOES SOUTH

The four-yearly Copa América tournament features all ten national teams from South America. Since 1993, other teams from North and Central America, such as Mexico and Costa Rica, have been invited to take part. Mexico has played in the Copa eleven times, more than any other guest, and even reached the final in 1993 and 2001. So far no one from outside South America has won the Copa América – that would be awkward!

JAN 16

TOP CATALANS!

Barcelona Femení won 62 league matches *in a row* between June 2021 and March 2023. The incredible run included the whole of the 2022 season, in which they won all 30 matches (scoring 159 goals and conceding just eleven) and the first 27 games of the 2023 season, until they drew 1–1 with Sevilla. Barcelona Femení had already won the Spanish league by then – and they went on to win the Champions League that season.

JAN 17

LOCAL LIONS

In 1967, Celtic became the first British team to reach the European Cup final – the forerunner to the Champions League – and caused an upset by beating Italian giants Internazionale 2–1 in the Lisbon final. Ten of the Celtic players had grown up within sixteen kilometres of their Celtic Park stadium. This band of locals was nicknamed the Lisbon Lions.

ON THIS DAY

JAN 18

UNITED TRINITY GET STARTED

Three of Manchester United's greatest-ever players – Bobby Charlton, Denis Law and George Best – played together for the first time on this day in 1964. They all scored in a 4–1 win at West Bromwich Albion and would go on to make history by guiding the club to 1968 European Cup success. They later had a statue built in their honour, which stands proudly outside United's Old Trafford stadium.

JAN 19

THAT IS SICK...

The word "vomitory" sounds disgusting, but it is a genuine word that is used by architects to describe the corridors that fans walk through when they enter or leave the stadium. The origin of the word is because the movement of fans in and out of the stadium (all one way, and then all the other) is just like the way food goes in the mouth one way and out the other when you vomit.

JAN 20

THAT IS SICKER!

Legendary French footballer Zinedine Zidane puked up on the pitch just before he was about to take a penalty during a crucial Euro 2004 game against England. The France midfielder put the ball on the spot and walked back before bending down and spilling up his guts. He then wiped his mouth and, four seconds later, took the penalty. He scored, and France won the game 2–1. Sick!

JAN 21

TRAINER FAINTS

In a 1930 World Cup match, a trainer passed out on the pitch and needed to be carried off himself! In the match between Argentina and the USA, the US team trainer, Jack Coll, ran onto the pitch to treat an injured player. But as he dropped his bag on the ground, a bottle of chloroform, a clear liquid used as a medical anaesthetic broke. He breathed the fumes … and passed out!

JAN 22

TUFT GUYS

Dundalk is one of the most successful sides in Ireland and the only Irish team to have ever won a match in the Europa League. On its crest are three martlets, which are mythical birds with tufts of feathers instead of feet. Not very good for playing football, you might think! The tufts, however, symbolize constant movement and continuous effort. No toes, no woes! No feet, no defeat!

JAN 23

LUIS IS ON FIRE

A top-division league match between Arsenal Sarandi and Gimnasia La Plata in Argentina was delayed for an hour in 2023 when a bird's nest near the stadium lights caught fire. The match eventually restarted and ended 0–0. The electrician who fixed the damage, Luis Mangou, was chosen as man of the match!

JAN 24

STARTING ELEVEN

Squad numbers first appeared on the backs of shirts in 1911, when Australian sides Sydney Leichardt and HMS Powerful wore numbers to help watching fans identify the players. Here are the shirt numbers generally played today (although they do vary).

GK goalkeeper
LB/RB left-back/right-back
CB centre-back
CM/CDM central midfielder/central defensive midfielder
AM attacking midfielder
LW/RW left-wing/right-wing
CF centre-forward

JAN 25

HAGGIS HERO

On this day in 1759, Robert Burns, Scotland's most famous poet, was born. Scottish people celebrate this every year with a Burns Night supper. They read his poetry and eat a traditional meal of haggis (a bit like a big sausage), neeps and tatties (Scottish for turnips and potatoes). It was also the day that a group of Scottish football fans founded Sevilla football club, the oldest in Spain that only played football. Sevilla's first president and captain were both Scottish.

JAN 26

FAN DABBIE COACHIES

Scotland has an amazing tradition of producing fantastic coaches. In the last 50 years, far more English First Division or Premier League titles have been won with Scottish coaches (twenty wins) than English coaches (twelve wins). Scottish coaches have also won four European Cups or Champions Leagues.

Coach	Club	Dates	League titles won	Year won top Euro trophy
Jock Stein	Celtic	1965–78	10	1967
Dave Mackay	Derby County	1973–76	1	-
Matt Busby	Manchester United	1951–67	5	1968
Alex Ferguson	Manchester United	1986–2013	13	1999, 2008
Kenny Dalglish	Liverpool	1985–91, 2011	4	-
George Graham	Arsenal	1986–95	2	-

JAN 27

WAT A GUY-ANA!

The first Black person to play international football was Andrew Watson, who captained Scotland in 1881 in a famous 6–1 away win over England. Born in Guyana, South America, to a Scottish dad and Guyanese mum, Watson came to the UK as a boy. He started playing football while at Glasgow University and quickly made the national side. He played for Scotland in two more matches (which they won) but was dropped when he moved to London. At the time, you had to live in Scotland to play for the team. Harsh!

JAN 28

GRAZIE, ROSE

Only one Scottish footballer has a World Cup winner's medal – playing for Italy! Rose Reilly played for Scotland in the women's first international match in 1972 but was banned by the Scottish FA after she criticized their attitude to the women's game. She moved to Italy, won two league titles and then played for Italy. In 1984, she scored in the final to help Italy win the Mundialito, an unofficial version of the Women's World Cup.

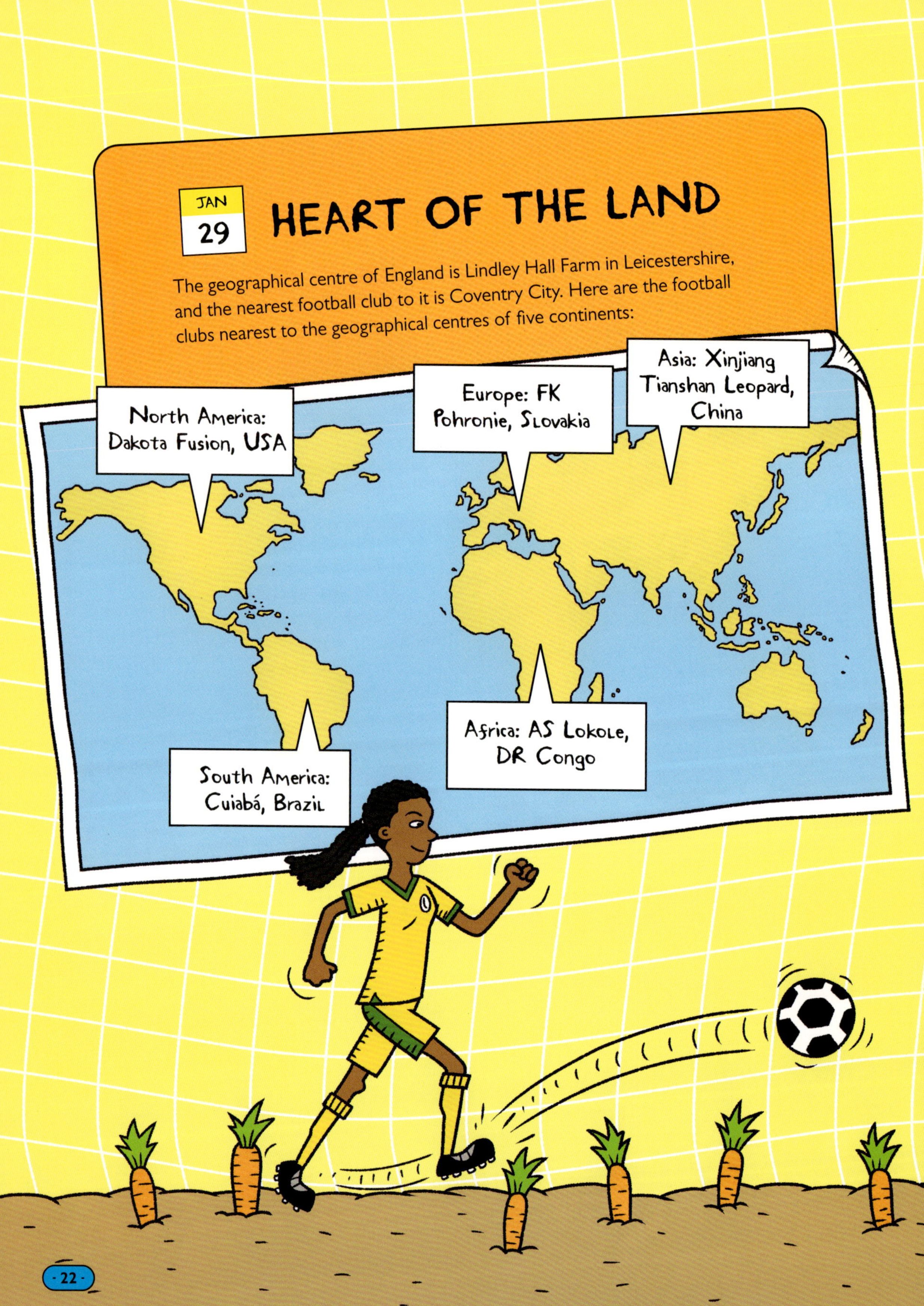
JAN
29
HEART OF THE LAND
The geographical centre of England is Lindley Hall Farm in Leicestershire, and the nearest football club to it is Coventry City. Here are the football clubs nearest to the geographical centres of five continents:
North America: Dakota Fusion, USA
Europe: FK Pohronie, Slovakia
Asia: Xinjiang Tianshan Leopard, China
South America: Cuiabá, Brazil
Africa: AS Lokole, DR Congo

JAN 30

THERE'S ONLY ... TWO BARCELONAS!

Many countries have clubs with very familiar names! Some of them have even won their national leagues.

ARSENAL OF LESOTHO
3 TIMES CHAMPIONS

EVERTON OF CHILE
4 TIMES CHAMPIONS

BARCELONA OF ECUADOR
16 TIMES CHAMPIONS

JAN 31

CARROT POWER

Jamaica striker Khadija Shaw was nicknamed Bunny by her brother because she loved carrots. The prolific forward, who became Manchester City Women's all-time leading scorer in 2024, is a legend in her home country. After making her Jamaica debut aged eighteen, she helped her country qualify for two Women's World Cups. She scored an incredible 50 goals in only 26 international games (a run that included four hat-tricks and one double hat-trick). She is still going strong. Powered by carrots!

JANUARY QUIZ

1. What links the national teams of Spain, Bosnia and Herzegovina, San Marino and Kosovo?

a) None of them have played in a World Cup final.
b) Their national anthems have no words in them.
c) They have all been coached by Serbian boss Bora Milutinović at some point.
d) They wear the same kit – red shirts and blue shorts – for home matches.

2. What Olympic event was hosted in 2018 behind one of the goals at South Korean side Gangwon's home stadium?

a) Surfing
b) Clay pigeon shooting
c) Skateboarding
d) Ski-jumping

3. Complete the following sentence correctly: England defender Lucy Bronze is the first female English player to …

a) … score in a major tournament with her left foot, right foot and head.
b) … win the Champions League with two different clubs.
c) … play in a position, left-back, that matches her initials.
d) … win a major tournament having been born in a different country.

4. How did the 1963 Scottish Cup tie between Airdrie and Stranraer make history?

a) Stranraer forgot their kit and didn't wear any shirts.
b) Both teams had an injury crisis and the game was played as seven-a-side.
c) The ball burst early on and the game continued using a rugby ball.
d) It was postponed 33 times.

5. How did Zinedine Zidane prepare to take his successful penalty in France's 2–1 win over England at Euro 2004?

a) He changed his boots.
b) He told the England goalkeeper where he was going to shoot.
c) He meditated for 30 seconds.
d) He vomited on the pitch.

6. How did Reading's lion mascot, Kingsley Royal, make history in 2014?

a) He was sent off because the referee thought he was a player.
b) He met Queen Elizabeth II at a Buckingham Palace garden party.
c) He spent the night in Windsor Safari Park with some real lions.
d) He was a real lion paraded around the pitch wearing a Reading kit.

Answers: 1. b, 2. d, 3. b, 4. d, 5. d, 6. a

FEBRUARY

FEBRUARY BIRTHDAYS
FEB
4
ALEXIA PUTELLAS
Spain midfielder, won the 2021 and 2022 Ballons d'Or and the 2023 Women's World Cup
FEB
5
CRISTIANO RONALDO
Real Madrid's all-time leading scorer and five-time Ballon d'Or winner
FEB
5
NEYMAR JR
Brazil's all-time leading scorer, Paris Saint-Germain (PSG) paid €222 million for him in 2018
FEB
8
JOSHUA KIMMICH
Germany star, won eight league titles in a row with Bayern Munich
FEB
8
ALESSIA RUSSO
Scored a semi-final, backheel nutmeg to help England win Euro 2022

FEBRUARY
FEB 18 ROBERTO BAGGIO
Won 1993 Ballon d'Or, missed Italy penalty in the 1994 World Cup final shoot-out
FEB 19 MARTA
Brazil's leading scorer of goals in World Cup matches, with seventeen goals in five editions
FEB 25 GIGI DONNARUMMA
Italy's goalkeeper hero when they beat England in Euro 2020 final on penalties
FEB 26 KAZU MIURA
Oldest player in the world, was still playing as a pro in Japan aged 56
FEB 26 JAMAL MUSIALA
Former England U-21 midfielder who now stars for Germany
FEB 29 FERRAN TORRES
Spain forward, born in the leap year 2000, so he only celebrates his birthday once every four years

FEB 1

SEEING RED

The Laws of the Game were rewritten in 1881 so that players could be sent off for "violent conduct" but it was not until 1970 that red cards were introduced so that other players, and fans, could see who was getting punished. English referee Ken Aston had the idea while he was waiting in his car at traffic lights at Kensington High Street in London. He knew that colour-coded cards could be easily understood by players and spectators.

FEB 2

TEMPER TEMPER

The most violent match of all time happened in the Copa Libertadores, which is South America's equivalent of the Champions League, in 1971. Boca Juniors of Argentina were losing the tie 4–2 to Sporting Cristal of Peru when Boca's captain sparked a massive brawl on the pitch. The referee sent off nineteen players and abandoned the match. The next day, all the dismissed players were handed 30-day jail sentences, but they were let off when Peru's government intervened.

FEB 3

GREAT DANES

Denmark won the first two Women's World Cups (at that point they were unofficial tournaments). The first World Cup took place in 1970, with Denmark beating hosts Italy 2–0 in the final. In 1971, over 100,000 fans watched Denmark beat Mexico 3–0 thanks to a hat-trick from Susanne Augustesen, who was only fifteen. Since then, their best World Cup performance has been reaching the quarter-final, which they last did in 1995.

FEB 4

FOR AND AGAINST

Jack Reynolds (1869–1917) was the first player to play for both Ireland (the home country of his mother) and England, where he was born. He made his international debut for Ireland against England in 1890, scoring a goal. Reynolds signed for West Bromwich Albion and, two years later, he was called up to play for England. He remains the only player to score goals for and against England (not including own goals).

FEB 5

NO DISTRACTIONS PLEASE!

When Argentina beat France in a penalty shoot-out to win the 2022 World Cup final, their hero was goalkeeper Emi Martínez. He distracted the French players by delaying the penalties, including slowly sipping water and throwing the ball to one side of the penalty area. These tactics contributed to two French players failing to score from the spot. After the game, football's Laws of the Game were changed so goalkeepers are no longer allowed to "unfairly distract the kicker".

FEB 6

BIRTHDAY BOYS

In any squad of 23 players, it is more likely than not that two players share the same birthday. But that doesn't explain the amazing coincidences of England's Euro 2024 squad. Midfielders Conor Gallagher and Adam Wharton shared a birthday on 6 February; attacking midfielders Jude Bellingham and Ebe Eze on 29 June; and defenders Kyle Walker and John Stones on 28 May (also Phil Foden's birthday). Not only were there three sets of shared birthdays, but the shared birthdays were of players in the same positions!

FEB 7

PALIN-DRAMA

A palindrome is something that reads the same forwards or backwards, like the surname of former Chile striker Marcelo Salas. A few players have had palindromic playing careers. Italy's 2006 World Cup-winning goalkeeper Gigi Buffon had one of the longest: he began at Parma, then played at Juventus, PSG and Juventus again, before returning to Parma. Front to back, and back to the front again!

FEB 8

THE FOOTBALL TIMES

SUPER CALEY GO BALLISTIC, CELTIC ARE ATROCIOUS

This famous headline was inspired by one of the biggest upsets in the history of the Scottish Cup, when in 2000 Celtic were beaten by part-timers Inverness Caledonian Thistle. The headline was top of the Poppins!

FEB 9

FAKE NEWS

According to research by American scientists, male players are twice as likely as female players to pretend to be injured during a professional match. Stop faking!

FEB 10

ONE-ONE WON!

These are the most common scorelines in English football based on a study of over 200,000 matches.

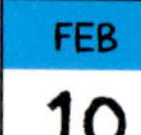

FEB 11

OLD BOYS

This is how the first-ever English Football League table looked at the end of its first season in 1889. All of these teams still exist, but not many are still in the top division!

Position	Club	Played	Points*
1	Preston North End	22	40
2	Aston Villa	22	29
3	Wolves	22	28
4	Blackburn Rovers	22	26
5	Bolton Wanderers	22	22
6	West Bromwich Albion	22	22
7	Accrington	22	20
8	Everton	22	20
9	Burnley	22	17
10	Derby County	22	16
11	Notts County	22	12
12	Stoke City	22	12

*2 points for a win

FEB 12

CHARLTON VERY ATHLETIC

In 1937, the French football federation needed to find an opponent for France at short notice, after their opponents, Italy, cancelled on them at the last minute. Belgium and Germany said no, so they asked Charlton Athletic, newly promoted to England's top division. Charlton had played a match the previous day, but jumped onto a night ferry and, the next day, beat France 5–2 in Paris.

FEB 13

CATCH OF THE DAY

The Mapei Stadium of Italian sides Sassuolo and Reggiana has a moat between the stands and the pitch – initially set up to stop fans running onto the pitch. Water from a nearby river flows into the moat, bringing fish with it.

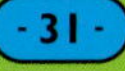

FEB
14
VALENTINE'S DAY
I think I'm in love with these facts!
That's one type of card I'm happy to get!
HOW ROMANTIC!
When striker Ashton Surber scored with a bicycle kick for Guam club Napa Rovers in 2017, he ran to the crowd, tearing off his jersey and going down on one knee to reveal the message "MARRY ME?" on his T-shirt to his girlfriend watching on. Before she had the chance to say yes (which she did), the referee came over and booked him for removing his shirt. No wedding invite for him!
MARRY ME?
MARRY ME
Norwegian winger Aron Dønnum took the brave decision to propose to his girlfriend midway through a fierce grudge match in Belgium between his team, Standard Liège, and rivals, Anderlecht. With Standard winning 3–1, the game was postponed after Anderlecht fans threw firecrackers onto the pitch. That did not deter Dønnum, who proposed to his girlfriend in front of a packed stand. She said yes! All the fans cheered as though another goal had been scored!

WINS HEART, LOSES GAME

In 2021, the coach of Paraguayan team River Plate Asunción found a unique way to propose to his girlfriend: he got his players to hold up placards with letters spelling out the words "Lili, Marry Me" (in Spanish) before a league game. Lili said yes, but her fiancé's mood soon worsened: his team lost the match 5–1.

TYING THE NOTTS

Angharad James and Amy Turner became the first British team-mates to marry when they tied the knot in 2021. James, a Welsh midfielder, played with Turner, an English defender, at Notts County, Orlando Pride and Tottenham Hotspur, where they became the first couple to play in the Women's Super League.

FEB 15

FLYING COLOURS

Most national flag colours are part of the kits of their national teams. Here are some exceptions.

Australia 

Japan 

Fiji 

Ghana 

India 

Italy 

Netherlands 

New Zealand 

FEB 16

ROSES ARE PINK, CHELSEA ARE BLUE

On the team bus on the way to the 2015 Women's FA Cup final, Chelsea coach Emma Hayes gave her players pink roses that she had grown in her garden and recited a poem by Rudyard Kipling, changing the last line from "you'll be a man, my son" to "you'll be a woman with wisdom". The gesture worked: Chelsea beat Notts County 1–0.

FEB 17

WHAT THE FLIP?

Before penalty shoot-outs were adopted in 1970, tied teams in knockout tournaments had to toss a coin to decide the winner of the draw at full-time. This happened in the 1968 European Championship semi-final, when Italy and the Soviet Union tied 0–0. The captains went to the referee's changing room for the coin toss. Fans only discovered the result when Italy captain, Giacinto Facchetti, ran onto the pitch, punching the air in delight.

FEB 18

BLUE TO RED

Anfield is the home of Liverpool, but it used to be the home of local rivals Everton! Everton rented the stadium there, moving out in 1892 because they didn't want to buy it. As a result, the landowner John Houlding – who was left with a stadium but no team – founded Liverpool to fill the gap.

FEB 19

MADRID DOUBLE

The 1980 Spanish Cup final had two familiar names competing: Real Madrid and Real Madrid reserves, known as Real Madrid Castilla. The Castilla side, made up mainly of teenagers, had beaten three top-flight sides to reach the final, which they lost 6–1. The rules have now changed to stop two teams from the same club playing in the same competition.

FEB 20

SUPER MÁRIO

Mário Zagallo was the first person to win the men's World Cup as a player and as a coach. He played in Brazil's successful campaigns in 1958 and 1962, then coached Pelé and his team-mates to glory in 1970 (he was also assistant coach when Brazil won in 1994). Only two others have also won the World Cup as player and coach: Franz Beckenbauer of Germany (1974 and 1990) and Didier Deschamps of France (1998 and 2018). Zagallo and Beckenbauer died within days of each other in January 2024.

FEB 21 — 1 TO 11

The starting line-ups of most teams include players wearing a shirt number of twelve or higher because their player shirt numbers are decided at the start of the season. Dutch club Sparta Rotterdam do it differently. Their line-up always wears numbers one to eleven so the players work out their numbers on the day of the match, depending on who is picked to play.

FEB 22 — COME IN, NO. 10!

Teams often retire shirt numbers in honour of club legends who have played for them. This is much more common in Italy, where you will never see these numbers at these clubs:

Shirt number	Club	Player
3	AC Milan	Paolo Maldini
4	Internazionale	Javier Zanetti
10	Roma	Francesco Totti
10	Brescia	Roberto Baggio
10	Napoli	Diego Maradona

FEB 23

SMALL IS BEAUTIFUL

The village of Loughgall in Northern Ireland has 280 residents, one street, one shop and a football team in its country's top division – the smallest place in Europe to achieve this.

FEB 24

HIJAB HERO

Morocco defender Nouhaila Benzina became the first player to wear a hijab in a World Cup match in 2023. A hijab is a head covering traditionally worn by Muslim women. It had been banned by FIFA until 2014. Her brilliant performance in a 1–0 win over South Korea has made her a role model for Muslim girls worldwide.

FEB 25

TWIT-TWOOOOO

"Where the owl sleeps" is the term used in Brazil to describe the top corners of the goal when a shot ends up there. In Spain, the term is "where the spider nests" and in England, it's "top bins"!

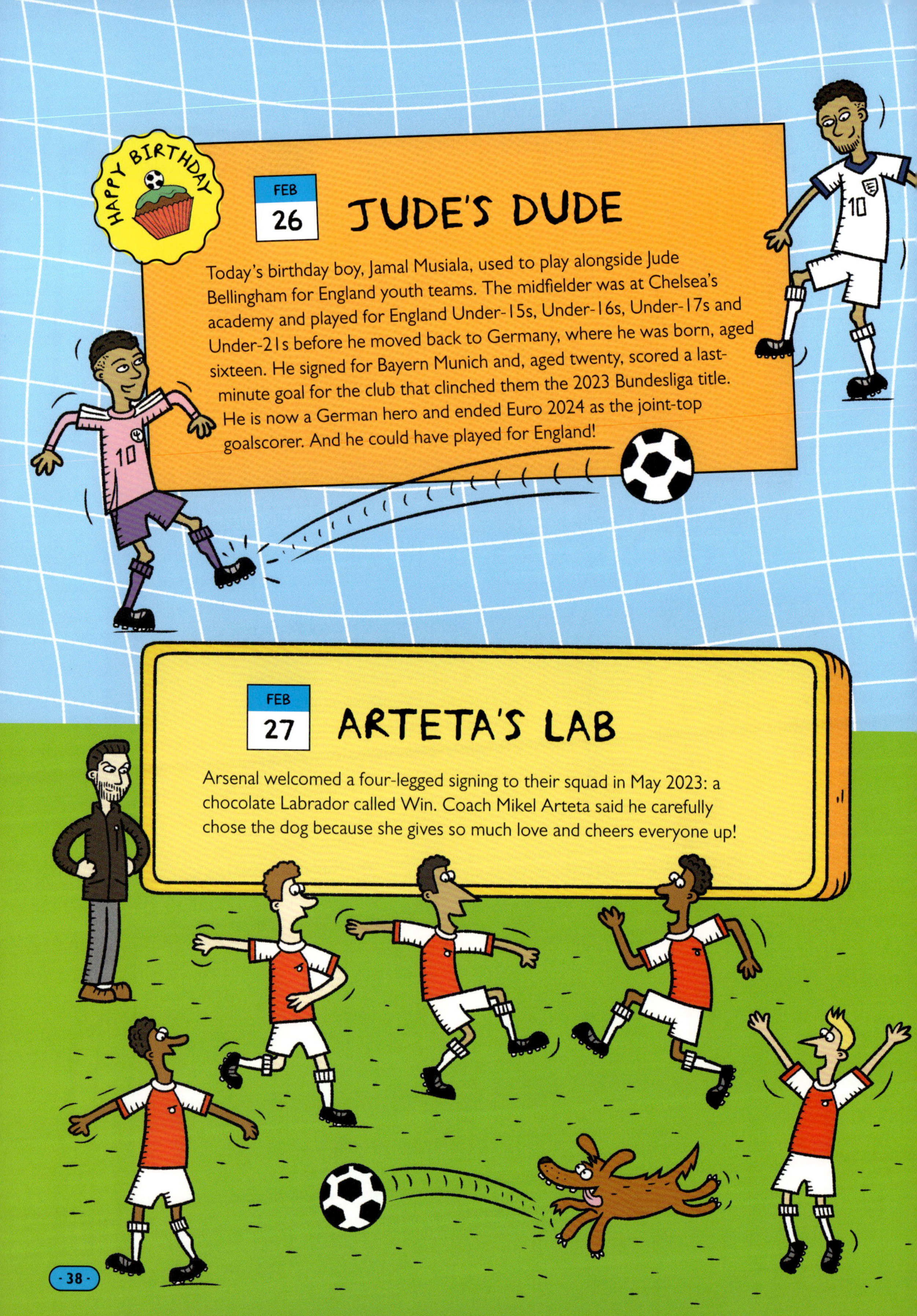

FEB 26

JUDE'S DUDE

Today's birthday boy, Jamal Musiala, used to play alongside Jude Bellingham for England youth teams. The midfielder was at Chelsea's academy and played for England Under-15s, Under-16s, Under-17s and Under-21s before he moved back to Germany, where he was born, aged sixteen. He signed for Bayern Munich and, aged twenty, scored a last-minute goal for the club that clinched them the 2023 Bundesliga title. He is now a German hero and ended Euro 2024 as the joint-top goalscorer. And he could have played for England!

FEB 27

ARTETA'S LAB

Arsenal welcomed a four-legged signing to their squad in May 2023: a chocolate Labrador called Win. Coach Mikel Arteta said he carefully chose the dog because she gives so much love and cheers everyone up!

FEB 28

NUTMEG, POR FAVOR

In England, passing the ball between an opponent's legs is called a nutmeg. The trick has other names in different countries.

Country	Name	In English
Austria	gurkerl	gherkin
Brazil	caneta	pen
Czechia	housle	violin
Morocco	bayda	egg
Netherlands	panna	gate
Portugal	cueca	undies

FEB 29

LEAP FOR JOY

Germany defender Benedikt Höwedes is the only player to win the World Cup after celebrating only six birthdays! Höwedes was 26 years old when he was part of Germany's 2014 World Cup-winning side (his header hit the post in the final) but was born on this day in a leap year, so is only able to celebrate every four years!

FEBRUARY QUIZ

1. Which country won the first two Women's World Cups in 1970 and 1971, before the tournaments were organized by FIFA?

a) Mexico
b) Brazil
c) Denmark
d) USA

2. What links the national teams of Ghana, India, Australia and Fiji?

a) Their home kits contain no colours from their national flags.
b) They have never had a player from their country score in the Premier League.
c) They have never won a tournament in the continent.
d) Their team mascots are all endangered species.

3. Which team used to play at Liverpool's stadium, Anfield?

a) Manchester United
b) England
c) Everton
d) Glasgow Rangers

4. Striker Ferran Torres was part of Spain's Euro 2024-winning squad, but what else made the year special for him?

a) He played for both Manchester City and Barcelona and won league titles with both.
b) It was a leap year, so he was able to celebrate his real birthday for only the sixth time in his life.
c) He became the father of triplets who were Barcelona's youngest-ever club members.
d) He was named the Spanish league's Player of the Month for five months in a row.

5. What is Jack Reynolds's footballing claim to fame?

a) He invented the idea of red and yellow cards while waiting at a traffic light.
b) He proposed to his girlfriend mid-match while playing for West Brom.
c) He won a competition to design Brazil's iconic kit.
d) He was the first player to score goals for and against England as he played for England and Ireland.

6. Which team finished top of the first-ever Football League table in 1889?

a) Preston North End
b) Aston Villa
c) Wolves
d) Blackburn Rovers

Answers: 1. c, 2. a, 3. c, 4. b, 5. d, 6. a

MARCH

MARCH BIRTHDAYS
MAR 7 RONALD ARAÚJO
Uruguayan centre-back who tackles hard
MAR 7 MARY EARPS
Inspirational England goalkeeper and Euro 2022 winner
MAR 17 MIA HAMM
USA's leading scorer and double World Cup winner
MAR 11 DIDIER DROGBA
Striker whose World Cup goals helped end civil war in his country, Ivory Coast
MAR 11 ANDY ROBERTSON
Captain of Scotland playing left-back. Won the Champions League with Liverpool in 2019
9

MARCH
MAR
9
PEDRO NETO
Portugal winger whose dribbling at speed terrifies defenders
MAR
8
WARREN ZAÏRE-EMERY
Exciting midfielder, scored on his France debut aged seventeen
MAR
10
NIKITA PARRIS
Won the 2020 Champions League with Olympique Lyonnais and Euro 2022 with England
MAR
24
WILLIAM SALIBA
France star known for his speed and calm composure
MAR
29
LEAH WILLIAMSON
England captain who lifted the Euro 2022 trophy
MAR
25
JADON SANCHO
England winger who reached the 2024 Champions League final with Borussia Dortmund

MAR 1

TAKE IT CLOSER

In 2010, there were almost thirteen shots from outside the box, on average, in every Premier League match. By 2023, this had fallen to only about eight – a drop of more than a third. One of the main reasons for this change is that coaches increasingly use statistical data to inform their tactics, and the data shows that there is a better chance of scoring if you take shots closer to goal.

MAR 2

DOUBLE TROUBLE

Only two coaches have ever won the World Cup more than once: Vittorio Pozzo (the birthday boy), who coached Italy's men's team to success in 1934 and 1938, and Jill Ellis, USA women's coach in 2015 and 2019.

MAR 3

SHE'S A GI-ANT!

Brazil midfielder Formiga played in a record seven World Cups. Her first appearance was aged seventeen in 1995, her last 24 years later in 2019 aged 41, an incredible feat of endurance and long-term fitness. Her real name is Miraildes Maciel Mota and Formiga is just a nickname, Portuguese for "ant", because of her intense focus and unselfishness.

MAR 4

THREE LIONS AND THEIR TAILS

England wear three lions on their shirt, and each of the lions has its own tale – or tail – to tell.

I came from King Henry I, who had a lion as his emblem when he was crowned in 1100.

I came on board when Henry I married Adeliza, whose father also had a lion on his shield.

I arrived in 1154 when Henry's son, King Henry II, married Eleanor of Aquitaine, who also had a lion on her family crest.

The next king, Richard I, often known as Richard the Lionheart, put all three lions on the royal crest, which the FA copied when they were founded in 1863. A roar-ing success!

CHEEKY CHIVAS

Being called the GOAT is high praise, because the letters stand for Greatest Of All Time. But in the past, not so much. In 1948, a reporter wrote that Mexican side CD Guadalajara had "played like goats" after a messy 1–0 win over Tampico. The club's fans loved the insult and took on the Spanish word for goats, *chivas*, as their nickname. Now Chivas de Guadalajara are Mexico's most popular and successful club. The goats are the GOAT!

NEW ENFANTS ON LE BLOCK

Paris Saint-Germain (PSG) is France's most successful team in terms of trophies won, even though the club is relatively young. It was only founded in 1970 and won its first Ligue 1 title in 1986, nearly 50 years after rival Olympique de Marseille won its first title.

KING OF PARIS

When PSG reached their first Champions League final in 2020, only two players in their 23-man squad were from Paris. They lost the match 1–0 to Bayern Munich, whose goalscorer, Kingsley Coman, comes from Paris and was once part of the PSG youth team. Awkward!

READY FOR THE TOP

HAPPY BIRTHDAY

In 2022, Warren Zaïre-Emery became the youngest player to play for PSG when he made his debut aged just sixteen years and four months old. One year later, he became France's youngest player for over 100 years, scoring on his debut against Gibraltar in the team's biggest-ever win, 14–0. He was part of France's Euro 2024 squad – but only after getting permission to delay his school exams!

MAR 9

VISA GEEZER

Serbian coach Bora Milutinović may be the most well-travelled international boss in history. He has been in charge of a record 287 international games. He achieved this feat by coaching eight different national teams: Mexico, Costa Rica, USA, Nigeria, China, Honduras, Jamaica and Iraq. He guided five of those teams at World Cups.

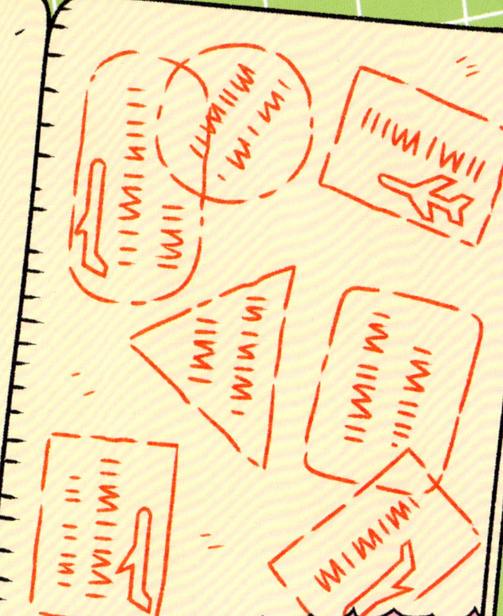

MAR 10

YELLOW ELTON

Pop star Sir Elton John is honorary life-president of Watford after owning the club in the 1970s, when they were in the fourth division, and helping them reach the first division. In 2023, Watford changed the road name next to the stadium to Yellow Brick Road. This was in honour of Sir Elton, linking to the name of his album *Goodbye Yellow Brick Road*.

MAR 11

PAWS OF THE GAME

Rule 3.7 in the Laws of the Game, the official rules of football, states that if "an outside agent" (such as a dog) enters the pitch and prevents a goal being scored by stopping the ball on the goal-line, the game is stopped. The referee restarts it with a dropped ball for the defending team goalkeeper in the penalty area.

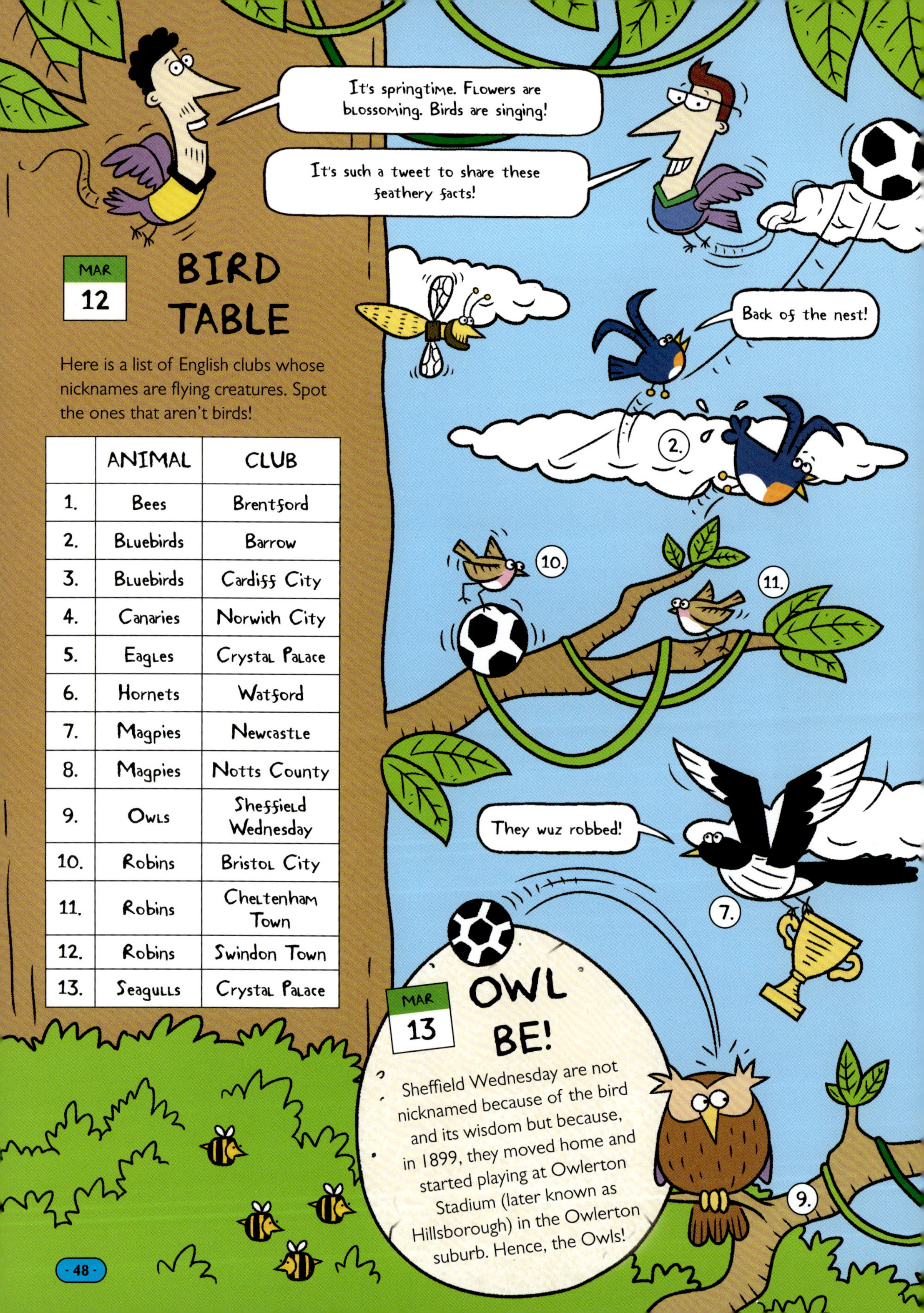

MAR 12

BIRD TABLE

Here is a list of English clubs whose nicknames are flying creatures. Spot the ones that aren't birds!

	ANIMAL	CLUB
1.	Bees	Brentford
2.	Bluebirds	Barrow
3.	Bluebirds	Cardiff City
4.	Canaries	Norwich City
5.	Eagles	Crystal Palace
6.	Hornets	Watford
7.	Magpies	Newcastle
8.	Magpies	Notts County
9.	Owls	Sheffield Wednesday
10.	Robins	Bristol City
11.	Robins	Cheltenham Town
12.	Robins	Swindon Town
13.	Seagulls	Crystal Palace

MAR 13

OWL BE!

Sheffield Wednesday are not nicknamed because of the bird and its wisdom but because, in 1899, they moved home and started playing at Owlerton Stadium (later known as Hillsborough) in the Owlerton suburb. Hence, the Owls!

MAR 14

SEAGULL STUFFED

Dutch club Feyenoord's club museum has a stuffed seagull in it. The reason? In a match at Sparta Rotterdam in 1970, Feyenoord goalkeeper, Eddy Treijtel, accidentally hit and killed the seagull from a goal kick. Feyenoord kept the dead bird.

MAR 15

SWANNING OFF

Danish club HB Køge are known as the Swans because the swan is Denmark's official national bird, and the Nordic symbol for looking after the environment. The club was also inspired by a fairy tale, *The Ugly Duckling*, as they hope to restore the club's fortunes, just as the ugly duckling turned into a beautiful swan.

MAR 16

KEET ON

Spanish club Espanyol are nicknamed the *Los Periquitos* (the Parakeets) because it is said that parakeets used to gather around the club's old stadium, and fans would feed them birdseed before games.

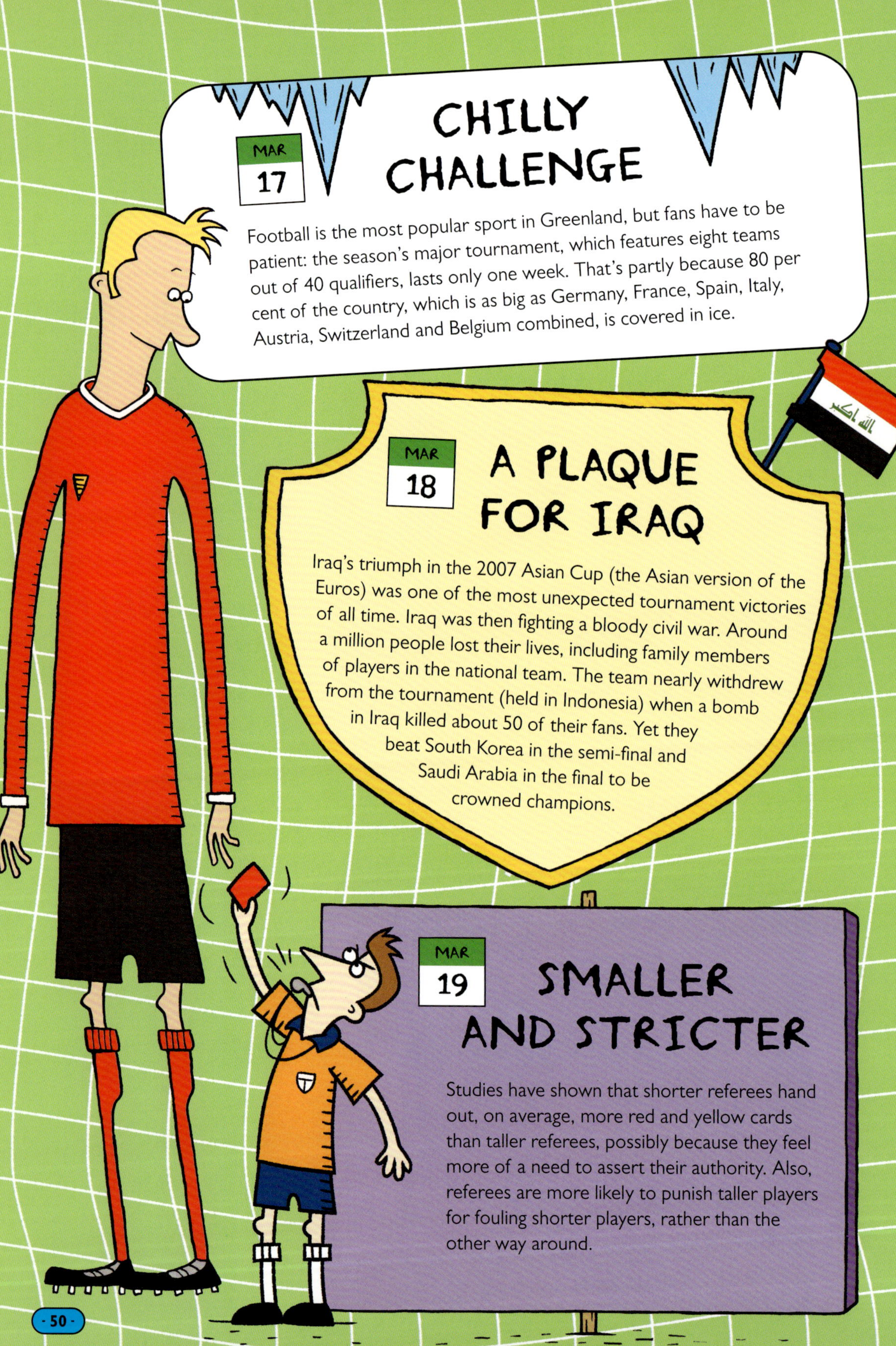

CHILLY CHALLENGE

Football is the most popular sport in Greenland, but fans have to be patient: the season's major tournament, which features eight teams out of 40 qualifiers, lasts only one week. That's partly because 80 per cent of the country, which is as big as Germany, France, Spain, Italy, Austria, Switzerland and Belgium combined, is covered in ice.

A PLAQUE FOR IRAQ

Iraq's triumph in the 2007 Asian Cup (the Asian version of the Euros) was one of the most unexpected tournament victories of all time. Iraq was then fighting a bloody civil war. Around a million people lost their lives, including family members of players in the national team. The team nearly withdrew from the tournament (held in Indonesia) when a bomb in Iraq killed about 50 of their fans. Yet they beat South Korea in the semi-final and Saudi Arabia in the final to be crowned champions.

SMALLER AND STRICTER

Studies have shown that shorter referees hand out, on average, more red and yellow cards than taller referees, possibly because they feel more of a need to assert their authority. Also, referees are more likely to punish taller players for fouling shorter players, rather than the other way around.

MAR 20

HOW DIVINE!

Here are five European gods and the teams named after them.

Ares, Greek god of war
Aris Thessaloniki, Greece

Thor, Viking god of war
Thór KA, Iceland

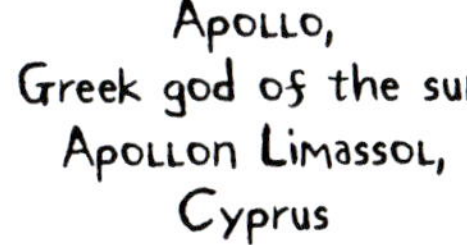

Apollo, Greek god of the sun
Apollon Limassol, Cyprus

Ajax, another Greek god of war
Ajax Amsterdam, Netherlands

Veles, Slavic pagan god
Veles Moscow, Russia

MAR 21

ATHLETIC BY NAME

Behind Real Madrid and Barcelona, Spain's third most successful club (in terms of trophies won) is Athletic Bilbao. What makes Athletic's success even more impressive is that since 1912, they have only selected players from their local Basque region, an area in the north of the country that accounts for four per cent of Spain's land and just six per cent of its population – a small but talented market!

MAR 22

TEEN-TASTIC

Only three teenagers have won the men's World Cup: the first was Pelé, who scored two goals aged seventeen when Brazil beat Sweden 5–2 in the 1958 final; next was Italy right-back Giuseppe Bergomi, who played in the 1982 final, a 3–1 win over West Germany, aged nineteen; and then Kylian Mbappé, who was also nineteen when his two goals inspired France to a 4–2 win over Croatia in 2018.

MAR 23

TEEN-TABULOUS

ON THIS DAY

Striker Endrick became the youngest player to score a goal at Wembley Stadium when the seventeen-year-old netted the winning goal in Brazil's 1–0 win over England in 2023. A few months later, he scored on his debut for Real Madrid, becoming their youngest foreign player to score a goal.

MAR 24

TEEN-SATIONAL

Northern Ireland winger Norman Whiteside was the youngest player to play in a men's World Cup. He was aged seventeen years and 40 days when he played against Yugoslavia in 1982. In the Women's World Cup, the record is held by South Korea forward Casey Phair, who was only sixteen years and 26 days when she faced Colombia in 2023.

MAR 25

THAT'S MY NAME...

Since 2022, the country formerly known as Turkey has been officially called Türkiye (pronounced Tur-key-yay). One reason for the rebranding was to avoid confusion with the bird turkey, traditionally eaten at Christmas, even though the bird was named after the country in the first place! Here are other countries, and their national teams, who have also changed names.

New name	Previous name	Year of change	Reason
Eswatini	Swaziland	2018	Avoid confusion with Switzerland
North Macedonia	Republic of Macedonia	2019	Avoid confusion with Greek region of Macedonia
Myanmar	Burma	1989	Make locals who used the name happy
Sri Lanka	Ceylon	1972	Country became a republic
Thailand	Siam	1939	Ruler wanted new national identity
Vanuatu	New Hebrides	1980	Break from old name given by foreign rulers

MAR 26

MAGNIFICENT SEVEN

Seven countries have appeared in each of the first nine Women's World Cup competitions, which started in 1991. They are Brazil, Germany, Japan, Sweden, Nigeria (the Super Falcons), Norway and USA. They have all reached at least one final, except Nigeria. Go, Super Falcons, you'll make it next time!

MAR 27

BACK-TO-BACK-TO-BACK

Bayern Munich became the first team from one of Europe's big five leagues (England, Spain, Italy, Germany and France) to win ten consecutive league titles when they clinched the Bundesliga in 2022. The European record remains at fourteen successive league titles for Skonto, Riga (Latvia, 1991–2004) and Lincoln Red Imps (Gibraltar, 2003–16), while the world record stands at fifteen titles in a row, courtesy of Tafea (1994–2009) from the Pacific nation of Vanuatu.

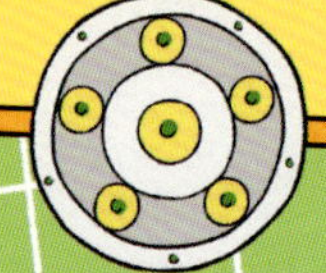

MAR 28

FAMOUS PERSON FC

Many clubs in Latin America are named after real people. Here are some examples:

Name	Country	Named after
CD Godoy Cruz	Argentina	Signed Argentina's Declaration of Independence in 1816
CD Luis Ángel Firpo	El Salvador	Famous Argentinian boxer from the 1920s
Club Jorge Wilstermann	Bolivia	The country's first commercial pilot
Club Presidente Hayes	Paraguay	19th-century US president, helped Paraguay after a war
Colo-Colo	Chile	Mapuche chief from the 16th century
Vasco da Gama	Brazil	Portuguese explorer who sailed to India

MAR 29

WHAT IS BORUSSIA?

Two of Germany's most famous clubs, Borussia Dortmund and Borussia Mönchengladbach, are based in the cities from the second part of their names. The "Borussia" comes from the Latin word for Prussia, a former European state that occupied a large area of what is now Germany, Poland, Lithuania and Russia. Prussia helped establish the Germany of today. That's why these two clubs, formed in the early 1900s, wanted Borussia in their name.

MAR 30

WALTZING TO VICTORY

The Australia women's football team used to be called the Female Socceroos. In 1995, TV viewers voted to choose a new name from a selection that included the Matildas, the Blue Flyers, the Waratahs and the Lorikeets. Because of the popularity of the Australian folk-song "Waltzing Matilda", the Matildas won the vote!

MAR 31

GAME OF TWO HALVES

Across the top five English leagues, there are more goals in the second half of a match than the first half. The split is 44 per cent in the first half compared to 56 per cent in the second. That's the nature of a game in two halves: in the second half, teams push harder for a goal and tired players make more mistakes. Substitutes make a difference, too, as well as injury-time, which is longer at the end of the second half.

MARCH QUIZ

1. What football record does Tafea FC, from Vanuatu, hold?

a) The fewest goals conceded in a league season, three, without winning the league
b) The first club side to provide a full starting eleven line-up for any national team
c) The only team to have never changed their kit since its foundation
d) The longest run of league titles (fifteen in a row)

2. Complete the following sentence correctly: Spanish club Athletic Bilbao …

a) … is the second most successful club, in terms of trophies won, in Spain.
b) … for over 100 years, have only selected players from their local region.
c) … wear red-and-white striped kits as their founders sailed to Bilbao from Sunderland.
d) … only appointed English coaches until the year 2000.

3. How long does the main football season last in Greenland?

a) One day
b) One week
c) One month
d) Six months

4. Match the South American clubs to the people they are named after

a) Vasco da Gama (Brazil)
b) Club Presidente Hayes (Paraguay)
c) Club Jorge Wilstermann (Bolivia)
d) Luis Ángel Firpo (El Salvador)

1. American president
2. Country's first commercial pilot
3. Argentinian boxer
4. Portuguese explorer

5. Which English king was the first to put all three lions on the royal crest, which is why the England team has three lions on their badge?

a) Henry I (ruled 1100–35)
b) Henry VIII (1509–47)
c) Richard I (1189–99)
d) Charles III (2022–)

6. Why is Sheffield Wednesday nicknamed the Owls?

a) Owls are wise and strong, like their players.
b) The club used to play in Owlerton.
c) They were founded by Lord Owle, whose name means owl in ancient Saxon.
d) Their fans have a unique chant in which they all hoot after a goal.

Answers: 1. d, 2. b, 3. b, 4. a) 4, b) 1, c) 2, d) 3, 5. c, 6. b

APRIL

APRIL BIRTHDAYS

1 FERENC PUSKÁS Hungary star, 1954 World Cup finalist	**2** ANDRÉ ONANA Cameroon goalkeeper, won trophies with Ajax, Internazionale and Manchester United	**3** GABRIEL JESUS Brazil forward, multi Premier League winner
8 KEIRA WALSH England star, Euro 2022 winner	**9** ROBBIE FOWLER England and Liverpool forward	**10** ROBERTO CARLOS Brazil free-kick specialist
15 FINIDI GEORGE Nigerian great, 1994 AFCON winner	**16** RAFA BENÍTEZ Spanish coach who guided Liverpool to 2005 Champions League success	**17** HORST HRUBESCH German Euro 1980 winner
22 KAKÁ 2007 Ballon d'Or winner, also the 2002 World Cup winner for Brazil	**23** CATA COLL Spain's 2023 Women's World Cup-winning goalkeeper	**24** STUART PEARCE Former England defender
29 DOMAGOJ VIDA Croatian defender, 2018 World Cup finalist	**30** MARC-ANDRÉ TER STEGEN Germany goalkeeper	

4 HARVEY ELLIOTT
Young English attacking midfielder
5 YASSINE BOUNOU
Moroccan goalkeeping great
6 JULIE ERTZ
USA Women's World Cup winner in 2015 and 2019
7 FRANCK RIBÉRY
French winger, nine-time Bundesliga champion
11 DELE ALLI
England 2018 World Cup semi-finalist
12 BOBBY MOORE
England's 1966 World Cup-winning captain
13 CARLES PUYOL
Spain 2010 World Cup winner
14 RAÚL BRAVO
Spanish 2002 Champions League winner
18 DONNY VAN DE BEEK
Dutch midfielder, Ajax title-winner
19 RIVALDO
Brazilian 2002 World Cup winner
20 LIV COOKE
British freestyle world champion
21 ISCO
Spanish five-time Champions League winner
25 JOHAN CRUYFF
Dutch coach, the most influential in history
26 LILY PARR
English record-breaking goalscorer and pioneer
27 HANNES HALDÓRSSON
Ex-Iceland goalkeeper and film director
28 DIEGO SIMEONE
Argentinian who won Spanish league titles with Atletico Madrid as player and coach

APRIL

APR 1
FOOLED YOU!
Football clubs love to play tricks on their fans on April Fool's Day.
Here are some silly ideas they announced on this day.
ARSENAL
Installation of a retractable sunroof on the top of their Emirates Stadium
LYON
Painting the grass on their pitch blue for the rest of the season
HARTLEPOOL
Playing in fancy dress for the last match of the season
That Hartle-fool-ed me!

SOUTHAMPTON
Addition of a smiley-face emoji to their official club badge
REAL MADRID
Going to launch a cricket team with Cristiano Ronaldo as a fast bowler
BAYERN MUNICH
Said that striker Zlatan Ibrahimovic was joining their basketball team
Did you know April in Spanish is Abril?
That's Abril-liant fact!
APRIL

APR 2

COUNTING THE SECONDS

How do refs decide how much additional time to add at the end of each half? They need to account for time lost through checking up on injured players, substitutions, time-wasting, yellow or red cards, VAR checks and goal celebrations, according to the Laws of the Game.

APR 3

FAR-SIGHTED

While you're watching your team play in one kit, designers are already planning the kit in TWO seasons' time! For big clubs, the design process can take around twenty months. It includes phases such as initial designs, creating samples and testing those with fans worldwide, before the mass production begins.

On sale 2029

SNAPPY TALE

The national team of East Timor, a mountainous-island country in Southeast Asia lying between Indonesia and Australia, is known as the Crocodiles. That's because the reptiles are sacred there. Legend has it that the country was formed after a crocodile turned itself into an island home for a small boy who had saved his life. Every bump on the crododile's back became a mountain.

APR 5

BOOTIFUL!

Sportswear brand Adidas' name comes from its founder, Adi Dassler, a German shoemaker whose boots with screw-in studs helped West Germany win the 1954 World Cup final. The match was played in pouring rain, and favourites Hungary took an early 2–0 lead. At half-time, the German players screwed in longer studs to improve their balance in the slippy conditions. West Germany won the game 3–2, Dassler then set up Adidas, and screw-in studs became widespread. Adi Dazzler!

APR 6

MATT OF ALL TRADES

Matt McQueen played over 100 games for Liverpool in the late-1800s and he played in every position on the pitch for the team – including as goalkeeper. After he retired in 1899, he became a referee.

APR 7

FOUR FOUR-TWOS

4–2 is the nineteenth most common result in football, but strangely it is the most common result in World Cup finals!

Year	Winners	Runners-Up	Score
1930	Uruguay	Argentina	4–2
1938	Italy	Uruguay	4–2
1966	England	West Germany	4–2
2018	France	Croatia	4–2

The most common result in Women's World Cup finals is 2–0, which is the fifth-most common result in football.

Year	Winners	Runners-Up	Score
1995	Norway	Germany	2–0
2007	Germany	Brazil	2–0
2019	USA	Netherlands	2–0

COOL TEAM

If you're looking for a cool team to support, try Finnish club Rovaniemen Palloseura (known as RoPS), who are based in Rovaniemi in Finland, about six kilometres south of the Arctic Circle. They have played in conditions as cold as –18°C. The Finnish season runs from April to October because the winter months are so cold and dark.

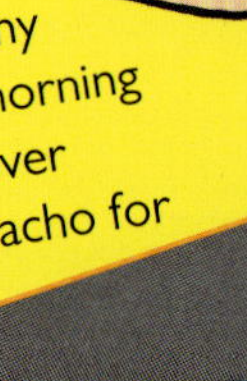

APR 9

WHAT TIME DO YOU CALL THIS?

In 2003, a Liga match between Barcelona and Sevilla started at 00.05 a.m. – the earliest-ever kick-off in a professional game. The game was set for midweek but the clubs had many other commitments. So Barcelona suggested Wednesday morning – at five minutes past midnight! Despite the sleepy hour, over 80,000 fans (each given a KitKat and cold soup called gazpacho for their support) watched the match, a 1–1 draw.

APR 10

PITCH PARTNERS

The following married couples both played for their national teams. They played for the same country unless marked.

Player	Player	Country
Danielle Egan	Claudio Reyna	USA
Jónína Víglundsdóttir	Haraldur Ingólfsson	Iceland
Malin Swedberg	Hans Eskilsson	Sweden
Ragna Lóa Stefánsdóttir	Hermann Hreidarsson	Iceland
Ruth Banda	Esrom Nyandoro	Zimbabwe
Sam Kerr (Australia)	Kristie Mewis (USA)	–
Sara Maglio	Steve Kindel	Canada

BANNED!

In April 1314, King Edward II banned football. "We command and forbid, on behalf of the king, on pain of imprisonment, such game to be used in the city in the future," he proclaimed. At that time, football was a totally unregulated game consisting of large mobs fighting each other for the ball.

APR 12

BAGGIES ON TOP

West Bromwich Albion's ground, The Hawthorns, is 168 metres above sea level, making it the highest professional ground in England.

AMERICAN SAMOA ERUPTS

Nicky Salapu was the goalkeeper for American Samoa when the tiny nation, made up of six volcanic islands in the southern Pacific, played in their first-ever World Cup qualifier in 2001. Salapu was the busiest player on the pitch, making over twenty saves as opponents Australia set a world record with a 31–0 win. Ten years and 30 consecutive defeats later, Salapu was the captain when American Samoa won its first-ever game, beating Tonga 2–1.

APR 14 POMPEY JOHN

John Westwood runs a quiet antique bookshop during the week, but at the weekend he transforms himself into Portsmouth's loudest and most recognizable fan. Westwood wears a top hat and wig, and gets the crowd going by playing a bugle and ringing a handbell. He has officially changed his name to John Portsmouth Football Club Westwood and even has PFC engraved on his teeth. Bet he celebrates his birthday with a Portsmouth-full of cake!

APR 15 MUMMY'S GIRL

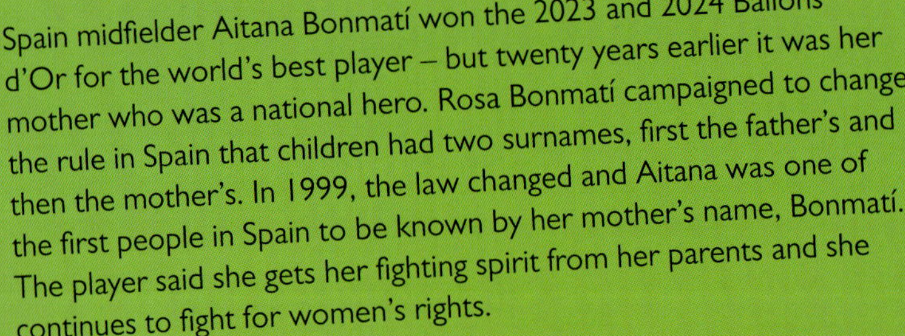

Spain midfielder Aitana Bonmatí won the 2023 and 2024 Ballons d'Or for the world's best player – but twenty years earlier it was her mother who was a national hero. Rosa Bonmatí campaigned to change the rule in Spain that children had two surnames, first the father's and then the mother's. In 1999, the law changed and Aitana was one of the first people in Spain to be known by her mother's name, Bonmatí. The player said she gets her fighting spirit from her parents and she continues to fight for women's rights.

APR 16 JOB FOR LIFE

Polish fan Paweł Siciński holds the world record for the longest single game of *Football Manager*, a computer simulation game where players pretend they manage a team through a season, making big decisions and competing for trophies. Paweł completed 520 seasons in which he managed 40 different clubs (and 80 national teams) and signed over 2,400 players!

APR 17 PIG POUCH

The world's oldest surviving football is a ball made from a pig's bladder, with a cowhide exterior. It is currently on display in a museum in the Scottish town of Stirling. It dates from the mid-1500s and was found behind the panelling in a bedroom in Stirling Castle once used by Mary, Queen of Scots.

APR 18 BALLS! BALLS! BALLS!

How many balls do you think could fit on one pitch? The world record is an incredible 142,393 balls, which took over 300 people to place at German club Borussia Mönchengladbach's home pitch in 2005.

APR 19 VIZ BIZ

The first leather footballs were brown, but in the 1950s, white balls were introduced so fans could see them under floodlights. In 1970 they changed to black and white so they were easy to see on TV screens. The Premier League has recently released three balls: one for summer, one for winter and a high-visibility one for snow.

APR 20 SECRETS OF SIALKOT

Over 1,000 factories in Sialkot, in the north-east of Pakistan, employ nearly 60,000 people to make most of the world's professional footballs. In one year, Sialkot produced 43 million balls.

APR 21

FORFAR 5 – EAST FIFE 4

Say this scoreline out loud – it is the most tongue-twisty result in British football. Fans of wordplay were overjoyed when a clash between the two Scottish second division clubs ended this way in 1964. They did it again in a 2018 Scottish Cup tie which ended 1–1 but went to penalties. The final score after spot-kicks? East Fife 4 – Forfar 5!

APR 22

MUSIC MAESTRO

One of Italy's most successful coaches, Giovanni Trapattoni, told his players that listening to the classical composer Mozart could improve their football. "You learn about tension, tempo, rhythm and structure," he said. Trapattoni won ten league titles in four different countries (Italy, Germany, Portugal and Austria), so he wasn't just blowing his own trumpet!

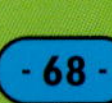

APR 23

ONE CLUB HEROES

Some players are celebrated for sticking with one club throughout their whole career. The most appearances for the same club was made by Brazilian goalkeeper Rogério Ceni, who played 1,197 matches for São Paulo between 1993 and 2015. He even scored 129 goals in that time! Here are some other players who showed the ultimate loyalty.

Player	Club	Dates	Appearances
Paolo Maldini	AC Milan	1984–2009	902
Billy McNeill	Celtic	1957–1975	790
Carles Puyol	Barcelona	1999–2014	593
João Pinto	Porto	1981–1997	587
Maria Gstöttner	USV Neulengbach	1998–2022	465
Jennifer Zietz	FFC Turbine	1998–2015	332

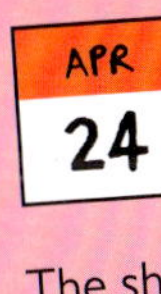

APR 24

SHIRT OF GOD

The shirt worn by Argentina captain Diego Maradona in the 1986 World Cup quarter-final against England is the most expensive football shirt in history. In the game Maradona punched the ball into the net, which he later referred to as the Hand of God goal, and he also scored FIFA's Goal of the Century, in which he dribbled past five England players to score. At the end of the game he swapped shirts with England midfielder Steve Hodge, who more than three decades later sold the shirt at auction for over £7 million. Now that's a decent swap!

LONG WAIT FOR GOALS

Australian midfielder Aiden O'Neill scored two goals in one game – but had to wait 156,956 minutes for the second one to go in! O'Neill scored for Melbourne City in their 2022 local derby against Melbourne Victory, but the match was abandoned after fans invaded the pitch. The match resumed four months later and O'Neill scored again to seal a 2–1 win. That was a long time coming!

THIS ONE'S A KEEPER

Willie McCrum was an Irish goalkeeper and amateur actor who felt that teams should be punished for fouls in the penalty area. In 1890, he wrote a proposal to football's lawmakers requesting penalty kicks. At first, people were furious at the suggestion that any fouls were deliberate and dismissed what they called "the Irishman's motion" (they thought he wanted goalkeepers to have more attention). One year later, after a controversial FA Cup tie in which a player punched the ball off the goal-line and no penalty was awarded, they reconsidered. So in 1891, the penalty was introduced into the Laws of the Game.

APR 27

CAMEROON ONESIE

Cameroon wore sleeveless shirts on their way to winning the Africa Cup of Nations in 2002 – but that kit was banned from the World Cup as FIFA wanted tournament branding to appear on the sleeves. Cameroon is no stranger to daring kits: in 2004, they wore onesies – all-in-one outfits that combine jersey and shorts. FIFA fined them as the rules state that players' kits must consist of separate shorts and jersey.

HE S-PFANNS THE GLOBE!

APR 28

German goalkeeper Lutz Pfannenstiel is the first person to have played for clubs in all six FIFA confederations, in a career in which he signed for 25 different clubs across thirteen different countries. That's a lot of new team-mates' names to remember!

KIT AHOY!

APR 29

Argentinian giants Boca Juniors play in blue and yellow because one day in 1906 the club bosses decided they would use the colours of the flag of the first ship that sailed into Buenos Aires, the Argentinian capital, on their kit. And the ship that sailed in that day was from Sweden, which has a blue and yellow flag.

TREES-Y DOES IT

APR 30

Austrian artist Klaus Littmann transformed the pitch of Austria Klagenfurt's 30,000-seater stadium in 2019 by planting 300 trees on the pitch. He wanted people to think about environmental destruction and the future of the natural world.

APRIL QUIZ

1. **Why does Argentinian team Boca Juniors wear blue-and-yellow kits?**
   a) To match the flag of Sweden.
   b) The colour combination is seen as a lucky one in Argentina.
   c) They were the only colours the printing factory had available when they requested a kit.
   d) Diego Maradona changed the kit to his favourite colours after winning the 1981 league title with Boca.

2. **Aitana Bonmatí has won the Ballon d'Or Féminin twice and the 2023 Women's World Cup for Spain. Why is her mum famous?**
   a) She was Spain's first female prime minister.
   b) She sang Spain's winning song in the 1998 Eurovision Song Contest.
   c) She was Spain's coach when they won the World Cup.
   d) She changed the law so children could be named after their mothers' surname.

3. **Whose football shirt sold at auction for £7 million?**
   a) Pelé's, from his first World Cup goal in 1958 for Brazil
   b) Sir Geoff Hurst's, from his 1966 World Cup final hat-trick for England
   c) Diego Maradona's, from the Goal of the Century and Hand of God in 1986 for Argentina
   d) Megan Rapinoe's, from winning the 2019 Women's World Cup final for USA

4. **What innovation did Northern Irish goalkeeper Willie McCrum bring to football in 1891?**
   a) Goal nets
   b) The crossbar
   c) Half-time change of ends
   d) The penalty kick

5. **The oldest ball in the world dates back to the mid-1500s. Where was it found before its current location, on display in a British museum?**
   a) In a bedroom in a Scottish castle
   b) In Sialkot in Pakistan, where most of the world's footballs are made
   c) In the away dressing-room loo at Wembley Stadium
   d) In King Henry VIII's tomb

6. **What world record does Paweł Siciński hold?**
   a) Has won the FIFA World Cup five years running
   b) Played the longest game of *Football Manager*, spanning 520 seasons
   c) Played the computer game *FIFA* for 100 consecutive hours
   d) Achieved the biggest win in *FIFA* gaming history after a 189–0 result

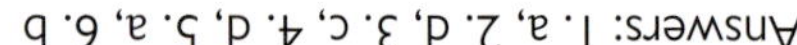

MAY

MAY BIRTHDAYS
MAY
2 DAVID BECKHAM
Former England captain, star midfielder and fashion icon
These players are all May-d in England
MAY
6 COLE PALMER
Winger who helped England reach the Euro 2024 final
10
MAY
9 ELLEN WHITE
England women's team all-time leading goalscorer

MAY
9
BETH MEAD
England striker and top scorer during successful Euro 2022
MAY
23
JOE GOMEZ
Defender who has played for England at every youth level
MAY
28
PHIL FODEN
England winger and multiple Premier League winner
16
2

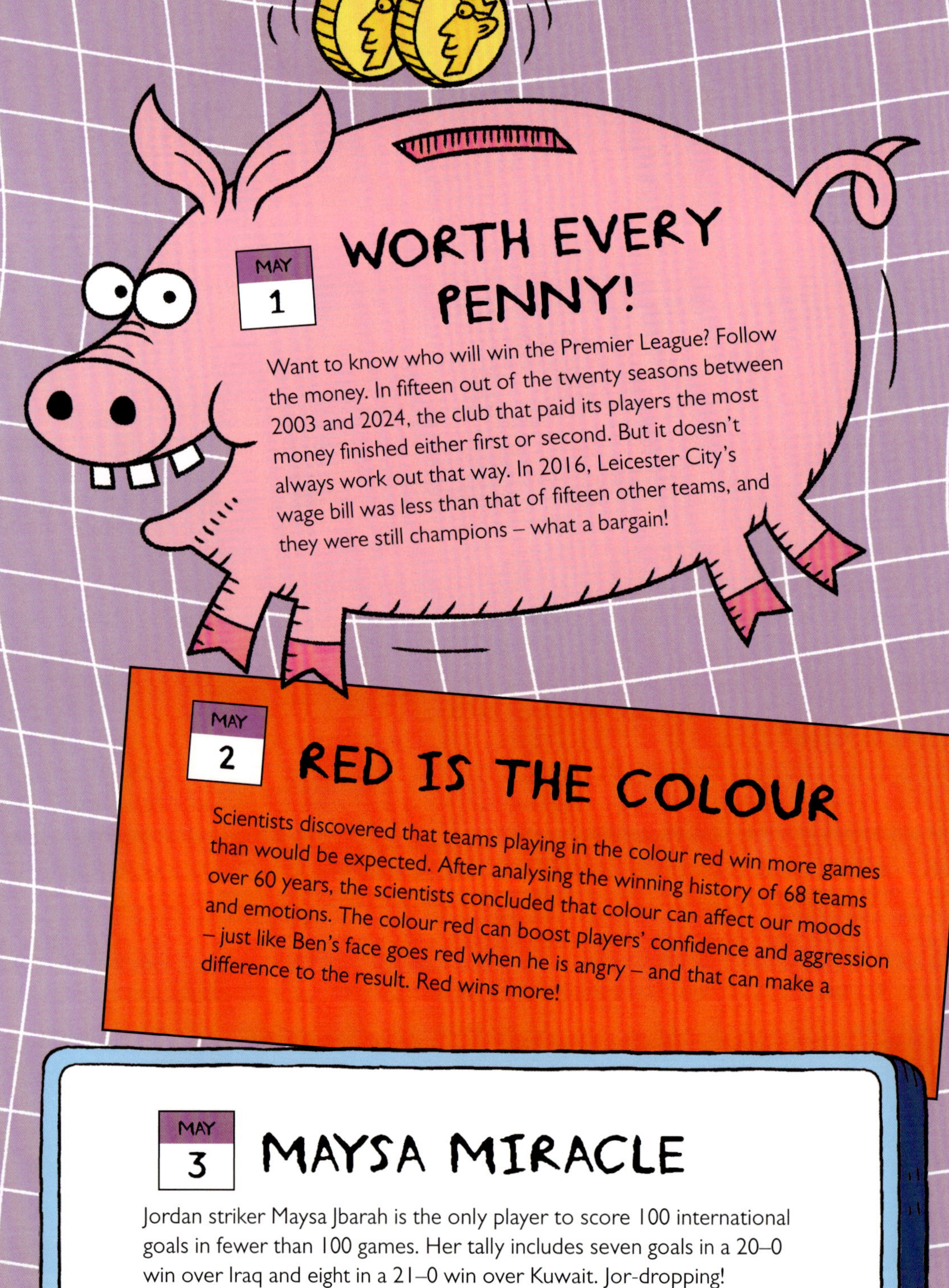

MAY 1

WORTH EVERY PENNY!

Want to know who will win the Premier League? Follow the money. In fifteen out of the twenty seasons between 2003 and 2024, the club that paid its players the most money finished either first or second. But it doesn't always work out that way. In 2016, Leicester City's wage bill was less than that of fifteen other teams, and they were still champions – what a bargain!

MAY 2

RED IS THE COLOUR

Scientists discovered that teams playing in the colour red win more games than would be expected. After analysing the winning history of 68 teams over 60 years, the scientists concluded that colour can affect our moods and emotions. The colour red can boost players' confidence and aggression – just like Ben's face goes red when he is angry – and that can make a difference to the result. Red wins more!

MAY 3

MAYSA MIRACLE

Jordan striker Maysa Jbarah is the only player to score 100 international goals in fewer than 100 games. Her tally includes seven goals in a 20–0 win over Iraq and eight in a 21–0 win over Kuwait. Jor-dropping!

MAY 4

DOUBLE TREBLE

Cameroon striker Samuel Eto'o has scored more goals than any other player in the Africa Cup of Nations, which he won twice. He was also the first player to win back-to-back European trebles when he won the Spanish league, the Spanish Cup and the Champions League with Barcelona in 2009 and the Italian league, the Italian Cup and the Champions League with Internazionale in 2010.

MAY 5

GIANT KILLERS

Here are some of the biggest upsets in world football.

By FIFA ranking
Faroe Islands 1 – Greece 0 (2014)
Faroe Islands ranking 187, Greece ranking 18
By population difference
Curaçao 3 – India 1 (2019)
Curaçao population 162,000, India population 1.38 billion (there is one person in Curaçao for every 8,438 in India)
By geographical area
Malta 2 – Canada 1 (2001)
Malta is 316 km^2, Canada is nearly 10,000,000 km^2

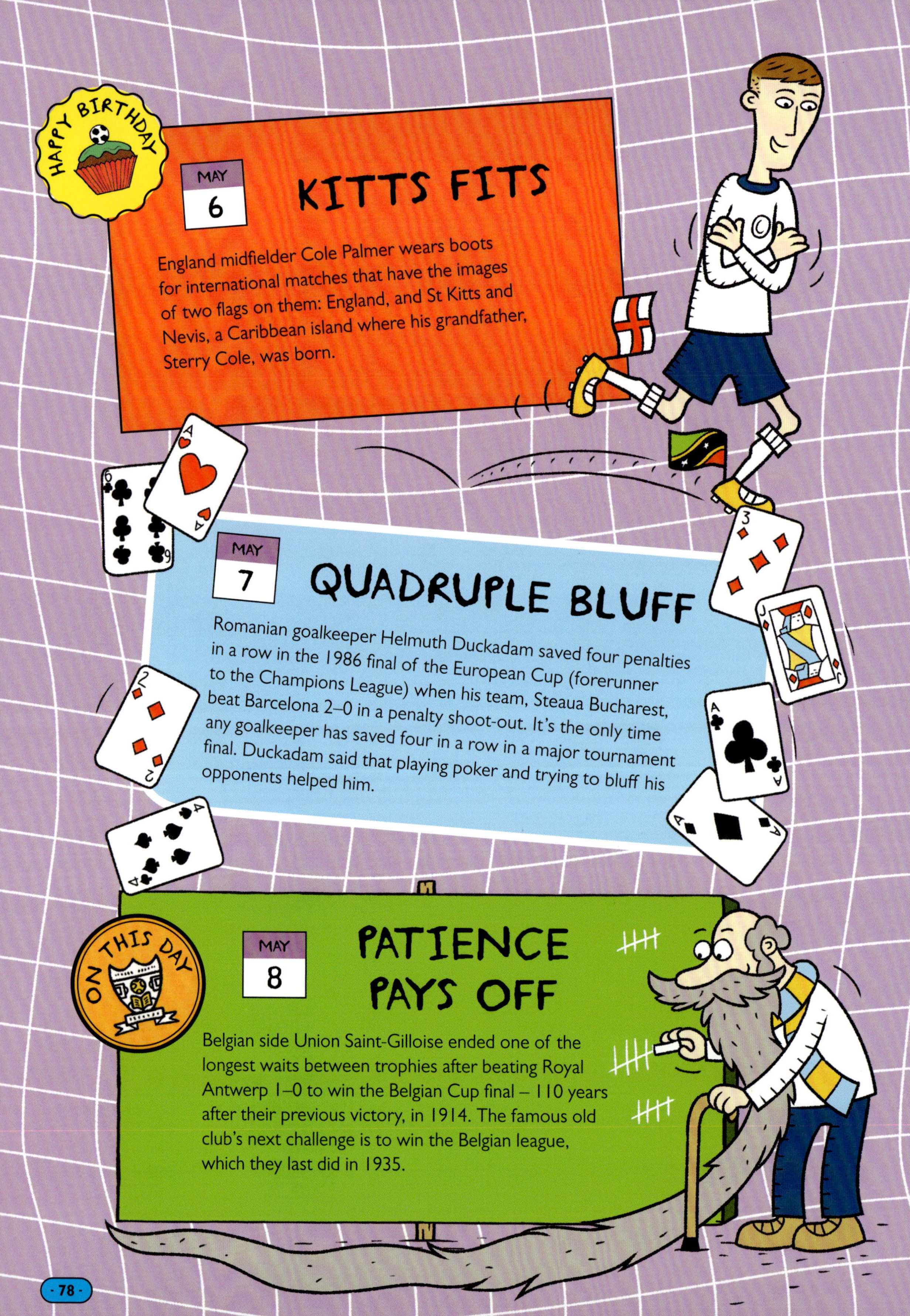

MAY 6

KITTS FITS

England midfielder Cole Palmer wears boots for international matches that have the images of two flags on them: England, and St Kitts and Nevis, a Caribbean island where his grandfather, Sterry Cole, was born.

MAY 7

QUADRUPLE BLUFF

Romanian goalkeeper Helmuth Duckadam saved four penalties in a row in the 1986 final of the European Cup (forerunner to the Champions League) when his team, Steaua Bucharest, beat Barcelona 2–0 in a penalty shoot-out. It's the only time any goalkeeper has saved four in a row in a major tournament final. Duckadam said that playing poker and trying to bluff his opponents helped him.

MAY 8

PATIENCE PAYS OFF

Belgian side Union Saint-Gilloise ended one of the longest waits between trophies after beating Royal Antwerp 1–0 to win the Belgian Cup final – 110 years after their previous victory, in 1914. The famous old club's next challenge is to win the Belgian league, which they last did in 1935.

MAY 9

SHOOT-OUT DISMISSALS

Only two goalkeepers have ever been sent off during a penalty shoot-out. The first was Botswana captain Modiri Marumo. He punched the Malawi goalkeeper Philip Nyasulu, who had patted Marumo on the shoulder following Malawi's third penalty. It was a quarter-final of the 2003 COSAFA Cup, a tournament for countries from southern Africa. Botswana lost the shoot-out 4–1.

The second happened in 2020, when Orlando City goalkeeper Pedro Gallese was shown a second yellow card for jumping early off his line in the 2020 Major League Soccer Cup play-offs. The rules state only the eleven players who ended the game can take part in the shoot-out, so centre-back Rodrigo Schlegel went in goal. He saved his first penalty and Orlando beat New York City. No keeper, no problem!

MAY 10

PERFECT DUET

Pop star Ed Sheeran is Ipswich Town's most famous, and possibly busiest, fan. He sponsors the club kit, has put money into the club's ownership group and, in summer 2024, he even helped recruit one player whose favourite musician was … Ed Sheeran. Just before he went on stage to perform with Taylor Swift, Sheeran telephoned the player and persuaded him to join Ipswich. The player must have felt "Shivers"!

'TIL DEATH DO NOT US PART

MAY 11

Brazilian club Corinthians has built a cemetery where there is room for the remains of 70,000 fans to rest. The Corinthians Forever Cemetery is for "fans from the beginning to the end".

GLOBAL GAME

MAY 12

The Premier League (PL) has hosted players from 126 different FIFA-registered nations. Since its launch in 1992, players from over 100 countries have scored. Notable players include:

Tanzania	Mbwana Samatta (Aston Villa) Scorer from country number 100 in PL list
Poland	Robert Warzycha (Everton) First foreign player to score in PL, in August 1992
Gibraltar	Danny Higginbotham (Man United, Stoke and others) Smallest nation represented, with an area of 6.7 km^2
Australia	Mark Schwarzer (Middlesbrough, Chelsea and others) Only non-UK player with over 500 PL games
Senegal	Sadio Mané (Southampton, Liverpool) Scored quickest PL hat-trick, in 176 seconds

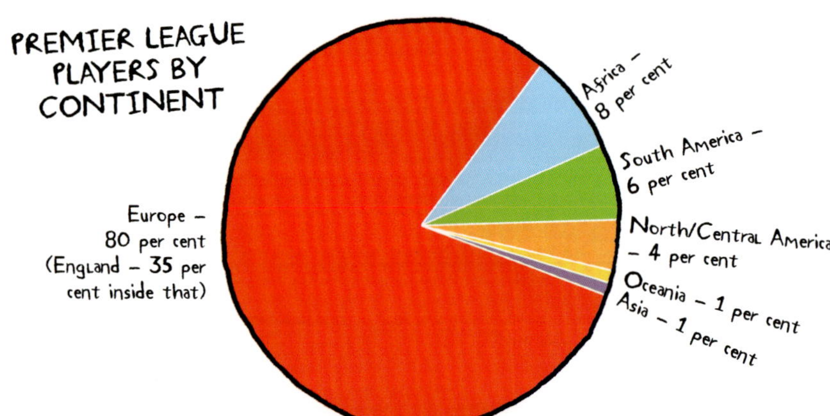

MAY 13

AGÜEROOOOOOO!

In 2012, Manchester City won their first Premier League title with practically the last kick of the season. They had to beat Queens Park Rangers to edge ahead of rivals Manchester United to the title. City were 2–1 down after 90 minutes, but equalized two minutes into injury time. Argentinian striker Sergio Agüero then scored after 93 minutes and 20 seconds to clinch the title. The commentator memorably extended Agüero's name in describing the goal by "Agüeroooooooooo!" and the number 93.20 is now famous for all City fans.

MAY 14

ARTFUL MIDFIELDER

Georgia Stanway discovered a new hobby after signing for German side Bayern Munich in 2023 – tattoo artistry! The England midfielder even inked a flower on the leg of her favourite Munich-based tattoo artist and friend, Linus Rüdel. Stanway says the skill is a helpful escape from the pressures of the game, and requires creativity, patience and composure – the same skills she shows on the pitch!

MAY 15

GAME OF TWO HEMISPHERES

The Zerão (Big Zero) Stadium in the Brazilian town of Macapá has the Equator running across the halfway line, so each half is in a different hemisphere.

THE WHITE HORSE FINAL

The first match Wembley Stadium ever hosted was the 1923 FA Cup final between Bolton Wanderers and West Ham. The final almost ended in disaster as over 100,000 ticketless fans turned up and thousands spilled onto the pitch before kick-off. The police pushed fans back with the help of PC George Scorey and his white horse, Billy, who safely coaxed fans off the pitch. Bolton won the game 2–0 but everyone remembered Billy, and the game became known as the White Horse Final. Fans have required a ticket for every final since.

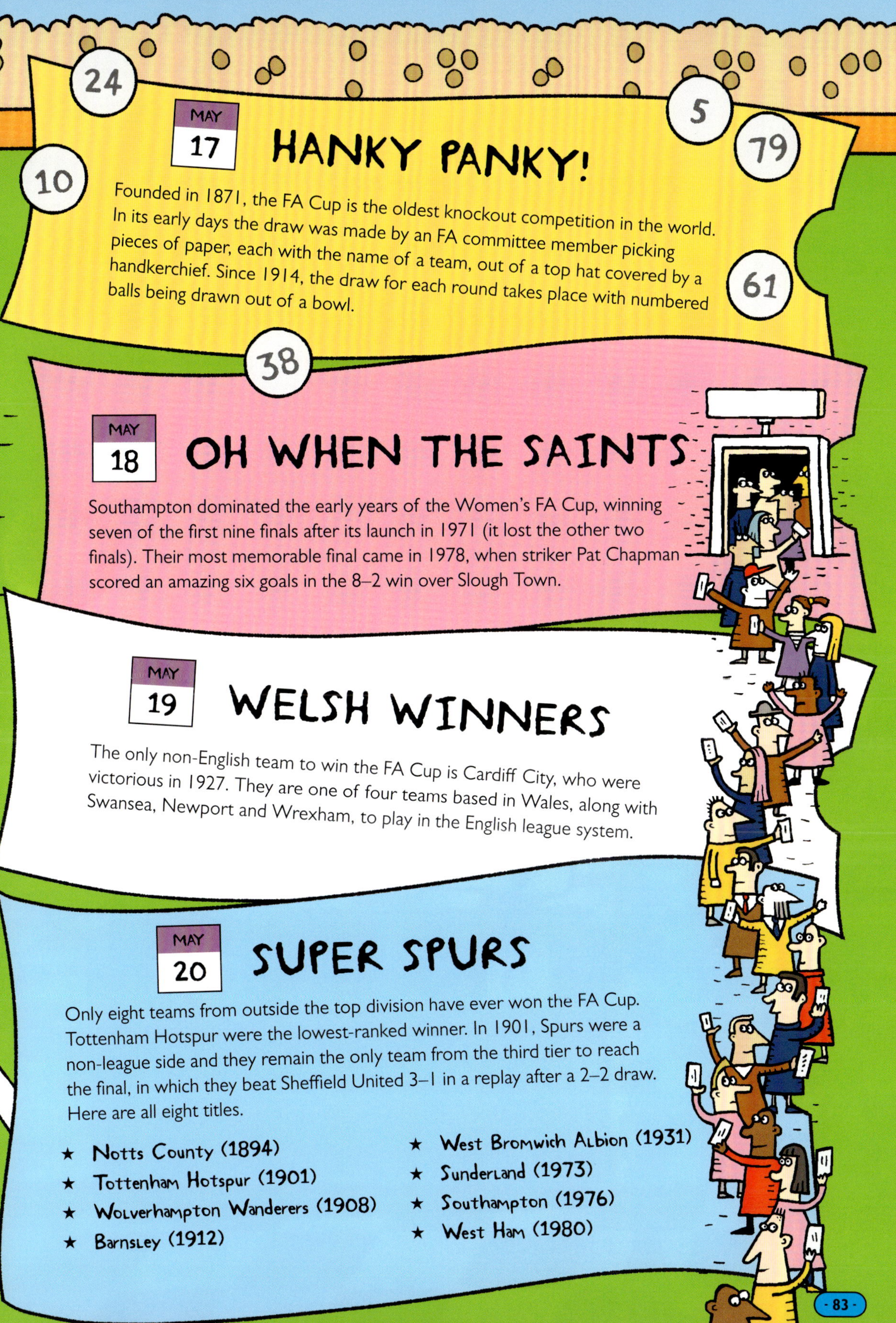

MAY 17

HANKY PANKY!

Founded in 1871, the FA Cup is the oldest knockout competition in the world. In its early days the draw was made by an FA committee member picking pieces of paper, each with the name of a team, out of a top hat covered by a handkerchief. Since 1914, the draw for each round takes place with numbered balls being drawn out of a bowl.

MAY 18

OH WHEN THE SAINTS

Southampton dominated the early years of the Women's FA Cup, winning seven of the first nine finals after its launch in 1971 (it lost the other two finals). Their most memorable final came in 1978, when striker Pat Chapman scored an amazing six goals in the 8–2 win over Slough Town.

MAY 19

WELSH WINNERS

The only non-English team to win the FA Cup is Cardiff City, who were victorious in 1927. They are one of four teams based in Wales, along with Swansea, Newport and Wrexham, to play in the English league system.

MAY 20

SUPER SPURS

Only eight teams from outside the top division have ever won the FA Cup. Tottenham Hotspur were the lowest-ranked winner. In 1901, Spurs were a non-league side and they remain the only team from the third tier to reach the final, in which they beat Sheffield United 3–1 in a replay after a 2–2 draw. Here are all eight titles.

- ★ Notts County (1894)
- ★ Tottenham Hotspur (1901)
- ★ Wolverhampton Wanderers (1908)
- ★ Barnsley (1912)
- ★ West Bromwich Albion (1931)
- ★ Sunderland (1973)
- ★ Southampton (1976)
- ★ West Ham (1980)

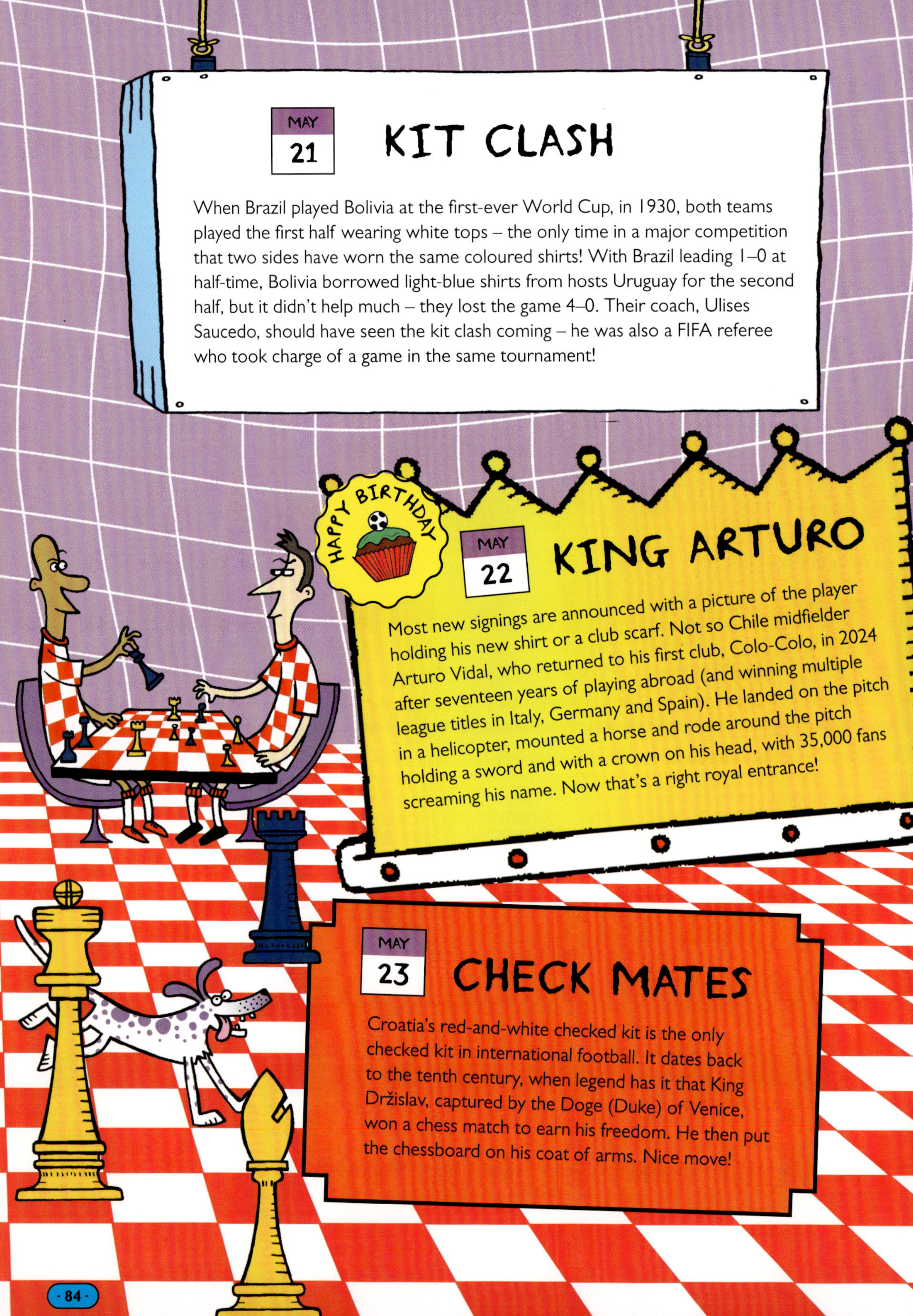

MAY 21

KIT CLASH

When Brazil played Bolivia at the first-ever World Cup, in 1930, both teams played the first half wearing white tops – the only time in a major competition that two sides have worn the same coloured shirts! With Brazil leading 1–0 at half-time, Bolivia borrowed light-blue shirts from hosts Uruguay for the second half, but it didn't help much – they lost the game 4–0. Their coach, Ulises Saucedo, should have seen the kit clash coming – he was also a FIFA referee who took charge of a game in the same tournament!

HAPPY BIRTHDAY

MAY 22

KING ARTURO

Most new signings are announced with a picture of the player holding his new shirt or a club scarf. Not so Chile midfielder Arturo Vidal, who returned to his first club, Colo-Colo, in 2024 after seventeen years of playing abroad (and winning multiple league titles in Italy, Germany and Spain). He landed on the pitch in a helicopter, mounted a horse and rode around the pitch holding a sword and with a crown on his head, with 35,000 fans screaming his name. Now that's a right royal entrance!

MAY 23

CHECK MATES

Croatia's red-and-white checked kit is the only checked kit in international football. It dates back to the tenth century, when legend has it that King Držislav, captured by the Doge (Duke) of Venice, won a chess match to earn his freedom. He then put the chessboard on his coat of arms. Nice move!

MAY 24

A TOUGH ONE TO SWALLOW

Frenchman Henri Delaunay's refereeing career ended when he swallowed his whistle – and broke two teeth – after a ball hit him in the face. Delaunay was one of the founders of the European Championships, which began in 1960. Ouch!

MAY 25

DROP 'EM AND RUN

Italian side Catania scored a goal against Torino in 2008 from a free kick after one of their players lined up in the wall … and pulled down his shorts to distract the goalkeeper. The tactic was the brainchild of Italian set-piece coach Gianni Vio, later part of Italy's winning Euro 2020 campaign. Vio claims to have over 4,000 free-kick routines in his database – most of which have players staying fully clothed!

MAY 26

ISLAND LIFE

Portsmouth's stadium, Fratton Park, is the only football ground in English professional football not located on the mainland; it's on Portsea Island, a small natural island which contains the city of Portsmouth. The stadium, though, is under threat from climate change. Experts have predicted that a quarter of English football stadiums are at risk of annual flooding or being underwater by 2050 as a result of global warming.

MAY 27

NAME THAT CONFEDERATION

The football world is divided into geographical areas by continent, with each region having its own governing body.

Area	Run by	Stands for	Countries
Africa	CAF	Confederation of African Football	54
Asia	AFC	Asian Football Confederation	47
Europe	UEFA	Union of European Football Associations	55
North and Central America Caribbean	CONCACAF	Confederation of North, Central American and Caribbean Association Football	41
Oceania	OFC	Oceania Football Confederation	13
South America	CONMEBOL	Confederación Sudamericana de Fútbol	10

MAY 28

IT'S ALL WHITE

Italian club AC Milan beat Juventus on penalties to win the 2003 Champions League final. AC Milan were wearing their all-white second kit for the game, which has brought them luck in the big European finals. AC Milan has played seven Champions League finals wearing the white kit and won six of them, compared to just one win out of four finals in their traditional, iconic red-and-black striped home kit.

MAY 29

FLAG IT UP

In the first Laws of the Game, written in 1863, there was no rule on the length or width of the football pitch. But the laws did state that each pitch should contain corner flags!

MAY 30

SPECIAL BOOTS

In 2020, Australian company Ida Sports launched a new football boot that was designed specifically for women's feet. Ida believes that the feet of men and women are different and, for too long, female players have worn smaller-sized shoes manufactured for male feet. The Ida boots are designed to allow for these differences. They include shorter studs (as women are lighter so do not need so deep a grip), extra support below the bones beneath the big toe, more arch support for the ankles, narrower heels and a wider toe area.

MAY 31

SAY WHAT?

In most languages, the word for football is either *football* or a word that sounds like it, like *futbol* in Spanish or *Fussball* in German. Here are some exceptions:

Language	Football
Croatian	Nogomet
Finnish	Jalkapallo
Greek	Podósfairo
Italian	Calcio

MAY QUIZ

1. What is Cardiff City's FA Cup claim to fame?

a) They have won the competition more times than anyone else.
b) They are the only non-English team to win the FA Cup.
c) They hosted the FA Cup final in the same year they won the competition.
d) The trophy was made in Cardiff.

2. Complete the following sentence correctly: Portsmouth's Fratton Park stadium is the only football ground in English football …

a) … named after a former player.
b) … to have hosted the Scottish FA Cup final.
c) … to allow dogs on the pitch.
d) … on an island.

3. What hobby did England midfielder Georgia Stanway take up to stay relaxed after she moved to Bayern Munich?

a) Growing vegetables
b) Life drawing
c) Astronomy
d) Tattoo artistry

4. What happened to Henri Delaunay, one of the founders of the European Championships, in his final match as a referee?

a) He swallowed his whistle.
b) He sent himself off.
c) He scored a goal.
d) He was beaten up by one of the coaches.

5. What special offer does Brazilian club Corinthians make its fans?

a) It gives a free Corinthians onesie to the newborn of every fan.
b) A Corinthians player will come to your wedding if you get married at the stadium.
c) It gives free Corinthians wallpaper to anyone who has moved house in São Paulo.
d) It has built a cemetery only for Corinthians fans.

6. What is unique about the FA Cup?

a) It's the oldest knockout competition in the world.
b) It's the only trophy to be made out of solid silver.
c) It's the only tournament in which a horse has scored a goal.
d) It's the only English competition that has been won by teams from Wales and Scotland.

Answers: 1. b, 2. d, 3. d, 4. a, 5. d, 6. a

JUNE

JUNE BIRTHDAYS

JUN 26 PAOLO MALDINI

Italy defender who said he only had to tackle if he'd made a mistake

JUN 24 DAVID ALABA

Austria star who won ten league titles playing for Bayern Munich

JUN 27 KHIARA KEATING

Youngest goalkeeper to win the English WSL's Golden Glove for most clean sheets aged nineteen

JUN 10 ONA BATLLE

Spain defender and 2023 World Cup winner

JUN 12 OLGA CARMONA

Scored winning goal as Spain captain in the 2023 Women's World Cup final

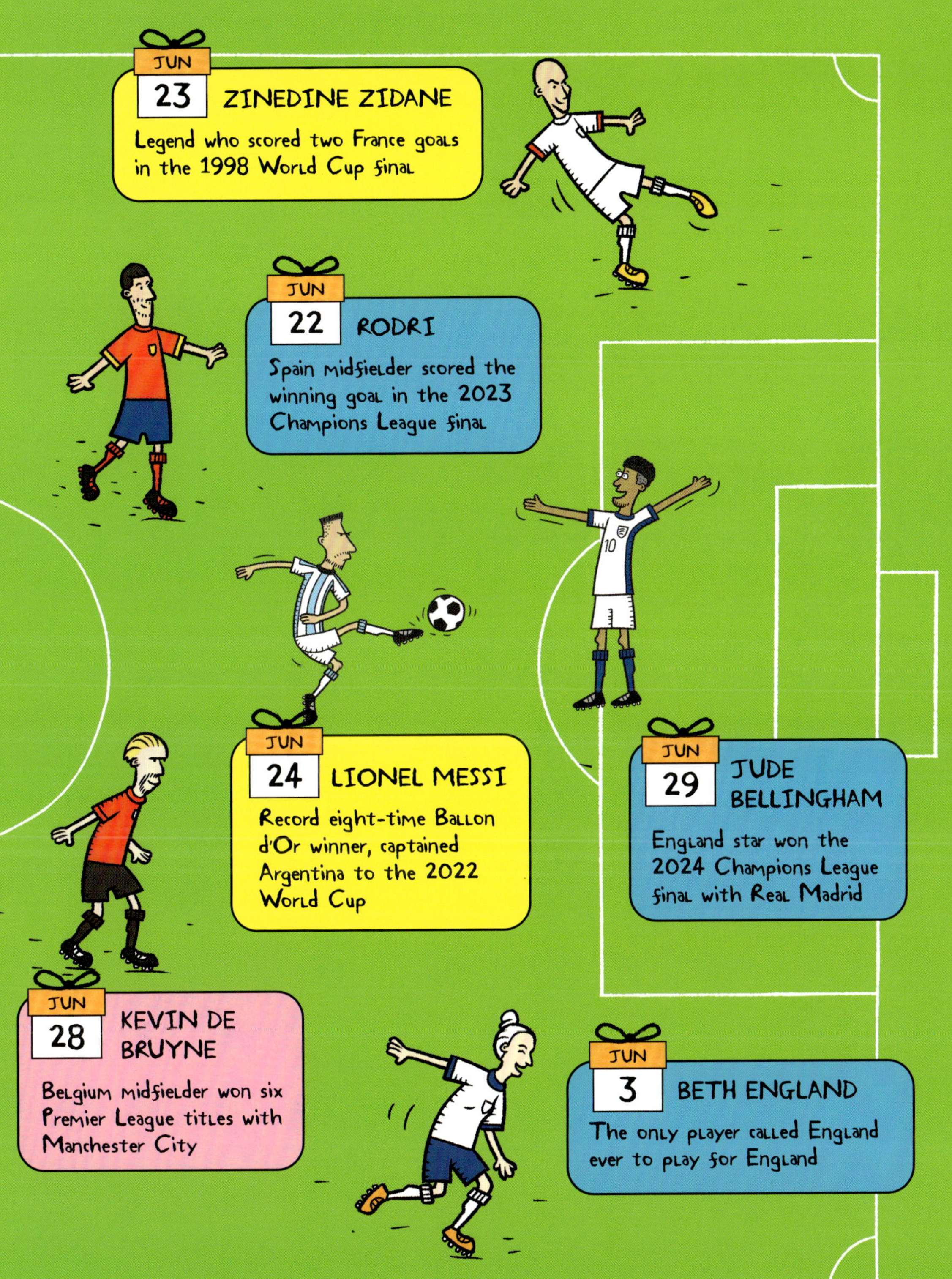
JUN 23 ZINEDINE ZIDANE
Legend who scored two France goals in the 1998 World Cup final
JUN 22 RODRI
Spain midfielder scored the winning goal in the 2023 Champions League final
JUN 24 LIONEL MESSI
Record eight-time Ballon d'Or winner, captained Argentina to the 2022 World Cup
JUN 29 JUDE BELLINGHAM
England star won the 2024 Champions League final with Real Madrid
JUN 28 KEVIN DE BRUYNE
Belgium midfielder won six Premier League titles with Manchester City
JUN 3 BETH ENGLAND
The only player called England ever to play for England

JUN 1 TRY AND TRY AGAIN

For those of us who are never going to be a world-famous coach, a rejection letter can be a trophy in itself. That's certainly the attitude of David Boyne, who has applied for over 150 jobs as a football coach but never got an interview – although he did get letters back from Chelsea, Arsenal, Manchester United, and even the England national team! Boyne holds the world record for most rejection letters received!

JUN 2 WE'LL HAVE WHAT THEY'RE HAVING

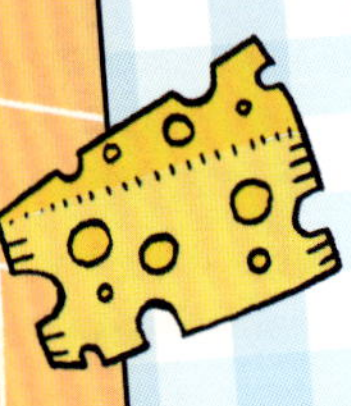

In the 1962 World Cup, Chile prepared for their matches by eating the national food of their opponents. They nibbled Swiss cheese before beating Switzerland 3–1, ate spaghetti before beating Italy 2–0 (played on 2 June) and drank vodka before beating the Soviet Union (Russia and its then linked countries) 2–1. What a menu!

HAPPY BIRTHDAY

JUN 3 SUM RUN!

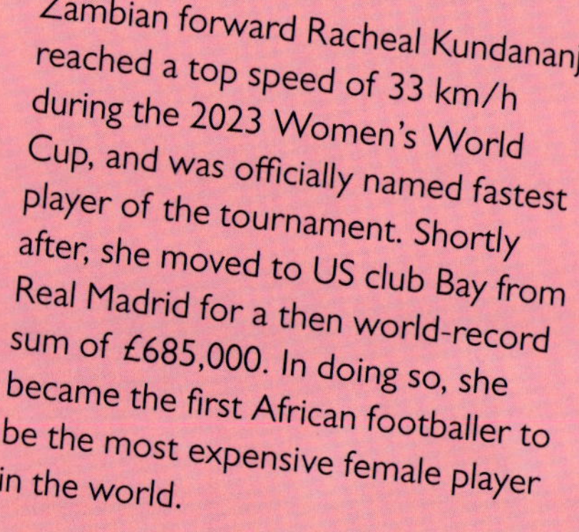

Zambian forward Racheal Kundananji reached a top speed of 33 km/h during the 2023 Women's World Cup, and was officially named fastest player of the tournament. Shortly after, she moved to US club Bay from Real Madrid for a then world-record sum of £685,000. In doing so, she became the first African footballer to be the most expensive female player in the world.

JUN 4 ROBINS IN THE HOOD

Suriname is a former Dutch colony in South America that is part of CONCACAF, the North American football federation, so that it can compete against Caribbean nations of a similar level. The most successful team in Suriname, Robinhood, was originally set up to give underprivileged youngsters a chance to better their lives. In 2024, they qualified for the CONCACAF Champions Cup, the North American version of the Champions League.

JUN 5 THAT'S LIT...

Jari Litmanen is the first player to have played international football across four different decades. The striker made his international debut for Finland in 1989. He played 137 times for his country (he also played for Ajax, Barcelona and Liverpool) and ended his career in 2010 – so played in the 1980s, 1990s, 2000s and 2010s. Jari good!

JUN 6 DOUBLE TROUBLE!

Belgium's Rik Coppens became the first player to score a legal goal with a "two-touch penalty" after the rules changed to allow it. This is when the penalty-taker rolls the ball a full revolution for a team-mate to run onto it to either score or pass. Coppens scored in an 8–3 win over Iceland in 1957. Here are some others who tried it.

First touch	Second touch	Team	Year	Goal
Cruyff	Olsen	Ajax	1982	Yes
Henry	Pires	Arsenal	2005	No
Messi	Suárez	Barcelona	2016	Yes
Neymar Jr	Icardi	PSG	2020	Yes
Cordova	Martín	Club America	2021	Yes

JUN 7

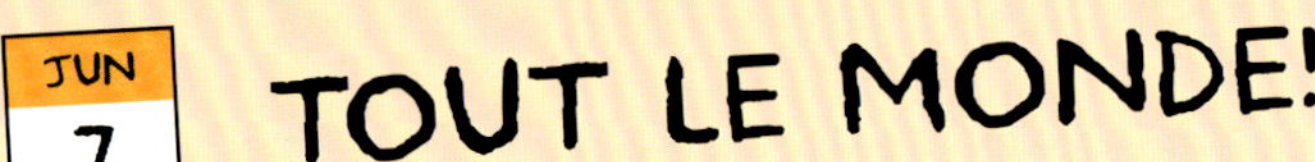

TOUT LE MONDE!

France produces more internationals than any other country – for nations other than France! An incredible 59 players at the 2022 World Cup were born in France – not only the 23 players in the French squad, but also players from Tunisia (ten), Senegal (nine), Cameroon (eight), Ghana (four), Morocco (two), Germany, Spain, Portugal and Qatar (one each). And at the 2023 Africa Cup of Nations, fifteen of the 24 teams had players born in France. Ooh la la!

JUN 8

THE TOOTH ABOUT BRAZIL

The Brazil national team that won the 1958 World Cup was one of the first to include non-football specialists in their squad. Brazil brought along a psychologist and a dentist for the competition, which they won. Perfect for big smiles with the trophy!

Goalie mouth action!

PENALTY COINCIDENCE

Germany goalkeeper Hans-Jörg Butt scored 37 penalties in his career, more than any other goalkeeper in European history. He scored three of those penalties in the Champions League, for three different teams: Hamburg (in 2000), Bayer Leverkusen (2001) and Bayern Munich (2009). On each occasion, Butt's opponent was the same: Italian side Juventus. No way, Juve!

JUN 10 GET YOUR STADION

The word "stadium" comes from the Greek word, *stadion*, which refers to an ancient unit of measurement, corresponding to the length of a running track. One of the most prestigious races in the original Olympic Games was a race that was one stadion long (around 180 metres). The race venue, which included seating for spectators, was also known as a stadion. Over time, the Latin version of the word, *stadium*, used by the Romans, was adopted for sporting venues generally.

JUN 11 DONKEY KAI

After Germany striker Kai Havertz set up an animal welfare charity and spoke about his love of donkeys, staff at a donkey sanctuary decided to name a fluffy grey-and-white foal after him. Kai the Donkey was born in 2023. Havertz's team-mates call him Donkey because of his love for the animals.

JUN 12 CANADA'S HERO

Christine Sinclair is the greatest international striker of all time. The Canada centre-forward retired in 2023 after scoring an incredible 190 goals in 331 Canada appearances. Her first was eight minutes into her first start against Norway when she was sixteen, and her last came 22 years later, against Trinidad and Tobago. In the intervening years, she played in six World Cups, and won two Olympic bronze medals before helping Canada win Olympic gold in Tokyo in 2021. Her secret, she said, was to hit the ball wherever the goalkeeper wasn't. Easy!

These two magic pages are all about goalkeepers...
Glove-ly!
JUN 13
MAGICIAN ON THE PITCH
Before the crucial fourth penalty in a shoot-out match in Mexico, Argentinian goalkeeper Nahuel Guzmán reached for something in his mouth. He then pulled out a strand of pink paper – then kept pulling and pulling. His party trick (which he learnt from clowns) took around 30 seconds to complete and left his opponent Ranko Veselinović waiting and distracted. The trick worked: Guzmán saved the penalty and his team won the shoot-out. Although he was booked for time-wasting!

JUN 14

EMI THE FROG

The prehistoric frog *Lepidobatrachus dibumartinez* is named after Argentinian keeper Emiliano "Dibu" Martínez (Dibu is a nickname). The Argentinian palaeontologists who found a fossil of the frog, which lived five million years ago, decided on the name because Dibu, the 2022 World Cup winner, was their favourite player. Hop hop hooray!

JUN 15

ABSOLUTE SCREAMER

Manchester United goalkeeper Alex Stepney once shouted at his defenders so violently that he dislocated his jaw. The game was against Birmingham City in 1975, when teams did not have substitute goalkeepers on the bench. In great pain, Stepney went off at the start of the second half, and midfielder Brian Greenhoff took over in goal. Amazingly, he kept a clean sheet and United won 2–0!

JUN 16

HANDY TO KNOW

In 1871, eight years after the Laws of the Game were made, reference to a goalkeeper was added – as a player who could handle the ball anywhere on the pitch. In 1877, that changed to handling the ball only in their own half. Then in 1912, goalkeepers were restricted to handling the ball only in their own penalty area.

JUN 17

KANGAROOS OF PRAGUE

When Czech team AFK Vršovice were invited to tour Australia in 1927, they had no idea it would lead to a new identity. As no one knew who they were, the Australian organizers suggested they call themselves Bohemians, as the Czech Republic used to be known as the Kingdom of Bohemia. The tour went well and the Australian hosts gifted their guests two kangaroos as going-home presents, which they brought back to Prague Zoo. Bohemians kept their new name and ever since have had a kangaroo, coloured green to match their kit, as their club badge.

JUN 18

STANLEY'S CORONATION

In 1953, many people bought their first TVs in order to watch the Coronation of Queen Elizabeth II. A month before the event, the BBC showed the 1953 FA Cup final – the first live major sporting event shown on TV in the UK. It was nicknamed the Matthews Final after Stanley Matthews, the Blackpool winger, inspired his team to come back from 3–1 down against Bolton Wanderers to win 4–3. Spare a thought for Matthews's team-mate Stan Mortensen: he scored a hat-trick for Blackpool but it was never the Mortensen Final!

JUN 19

ENGLAND RESERVED ABOUT SUBS

Studies have shown that coaches in Spain and Italy's top leagues use the most substitutes, and make substitutions earlier in games than in other leagues. Out of the top five leagues (England, France, Germany, Italy, Spain) use of substitutes is lowest in England's Premier League, with teams using all five subs in a game around only 34 per cent of the time.

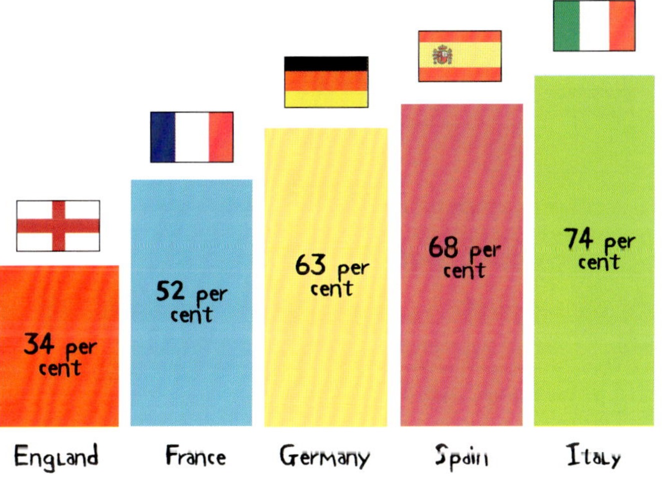

JUN 20

FAÉ'S FAB PHASE

Emerse Faé had never coached a senior football match in his life until he was brought in to coach Ivory Coast midway through the 2023 Africa Cup of Nations. The Ivorians were hosting the tournament, but lost two of their three group games. They assumed they would be eliminated and so sacked their coach. Then a series of results in other matches allowed them to qualify for the next round, with Faé in charge. They won that round on penalties, won the quarter-final with a last-minute winner, and beat DR Congo in the semi-final. Ivory Coast beat Nigeria 2–1 in the final, leaving new coach Faé with a 100 per cent record, and the title of national hero!

JUN 21

NO MEN ALLOWED

Two Brazilian teams made history when fans were banned from their stadiums for three matches as punishment for a brawl in 2022. The clubs, Coritiba and Athletico Paranaense, asked the court to reconsider and allow women and children in as they had played no part in the trouble. The court agreed: Coritiba hosted 9,000 women and children for their home match and Paranaense hosted 32,000 and 37,000 women and children for their matches. They all loved the atmosphere!

JUN 22

WORLD RECORD TRANSFERS

The first player who moved for a transfer fee was Willie Groves, who moved from West Bromwich Albion to Aston Villa for £100 in 1893. Since then, transfer fees have gone up and up. Here are some records.

Year	Player	From	To	Fee
1905	Alf Common	Sunderland	Middlesbrough	€1,000
1975	Guiseppe Savoldi	Bologna	Napoli	€1.2 million
1992	Jean-Pierre Papin	Marseille	AC Milan	€10 million
2013	Gareth Bale	Tottenham	Real Madrid	€85 million
2017	Neymar Jr	Barcelona	PSG	€200 million

JUN
23

MOO-TIFUL GAME!

Paraguay has two main languages: Spanish and Guarani, a language understood by 77 per cent of the population. The Guarani word for football is *vakapipopo*, which translates as "bouncing cow skin". *Vaka* means cow, *pi* means skin and *popo* means bouncing. Literally!

JUN
24

HAPPY BIRTHDAY

HOW MESSI SCORES HIS GOALS

Lionel Messi's 672 goals for Barcelona are more than anyone has scored for one club before. Messi scores the vast majority of his goals with his left foot. This pie chart shows the breakdown from his total of 850 goals scored for Barcelona, Inter Miami and the Argentina national team (up to 1 February 2025).

HOW MESSI SCORES

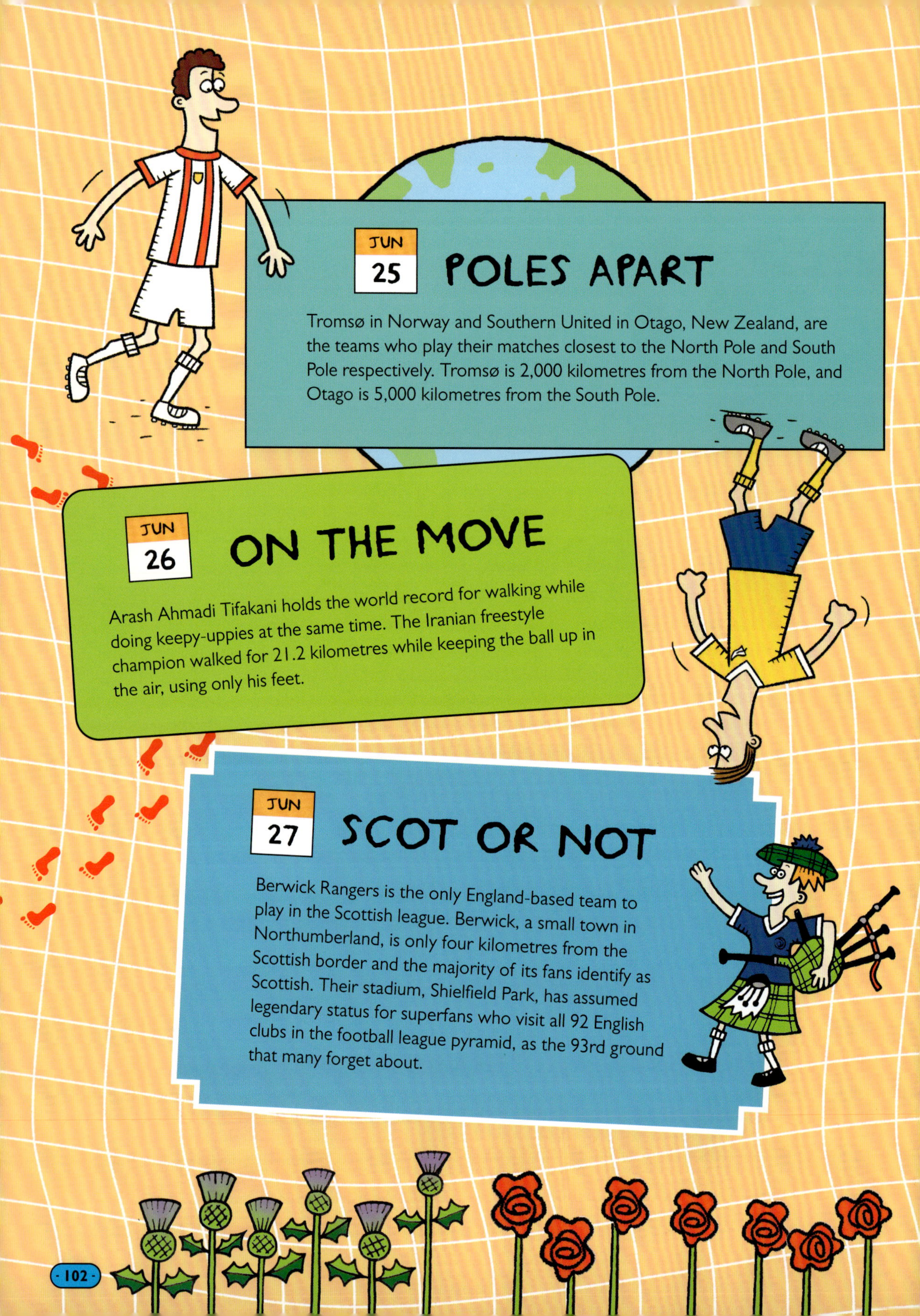

JUN 25

POLES APART

Tromsø in Norway and Southern United in Otago, New Zealand, are the teams who play their matches closest to the North Pole and South Pole respectively. Tromsø is 2,000 kilometres from the North Pole, and Otago is 5,000 kilometres from the South Pole.

JUN 26

ON THE MOVE

Arash Ahmadi Tifakani holds the world record for walking while doing keepy-uppies at the same time. The Iranian freestyle champion walked for 21.2 kilometres while keeping the ball up in the air, using only his feet.

JUN 27

SCOT OR NOT

Berwick Rangers is the only England-based team to play in the Scottish league. Berwick, a small town in Northumberland, is only four kilometres from the Scottish border and the majority of its fans identify as Scottish. Their stadium, Shielfield Park, has assumed legendary status for superfans who visit all 92 English clubs in the football league pyramid, as the 93rd ground that many forget about.

JUN 28

PAINT MARKS

Clubs use up to 2,000 litres of paint to mark out training pitches during one season. That's a lotta litres!

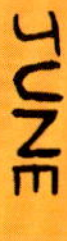

JUN 29

HEY JUDE!

Jude Bellingham played for Birmingham City for one season, wearing the number 22 shirt. When the England star left the club in 2020, the club retired the 22 shirt, meaning no other player can now use it. They thought no one would come close to being as good as he was. Bellingham wore the number 22 because he could play as a four, eight and ten all rolled into one player. Add 4+8+10 together and you get 22! He's 2, 2 good!

JUN 30

SQUASH THE BALL

For a ball to be certified as FIFA quality, it needs to pass seven tests relating to size, shape, bounce, water absorption, weight, pressure loss and shape retention. In the water absorption test, the ball is squashed 250 times in a machine half filled with water to check it does not absorb more than 10 per cent of its weight in water.

JUNE QUIZ

1. **In 2024, what was Zambian forward Racheal Kundananji's notable achievement at the 2023 Women's World Cup?**
   a) First goalscorer
   b) Fastest player
   c) Top scorer
   d) Only player to score a goal and save a penalty

2. **What other national team did England's Cole Palmer qualify to play for?**
   a) St Kitts and Nevis
   b) Grenada
   c) St Lucia
   d) Barbados

3. **Complete the following sentence correctly: *Lepidobatrachus dibumartinez*, named after Argentinian goalkeeper "Dibu" Martínez, is …**
   a) … a medical condition associated with hyperactivity.
   b) … an award-winning poem written by Argentina's most famous poet.
   c) … a winter car tyre with special grip for icy conditions.
   d) … a prehistoric frog.

4. **Why did so many people watch the 1953 FA Cup final?**
   a) They had bought their first TVs to watch the Coronation of Queen Elizabeth II shortly after.
   b) It was broadcast live in local cinemas across the country.
   c) Entry at the stadium was free, so the crowd tripled in size.
   d) Because it was before the invention of the penalty shoot-out, and there were six replays after six "finals" ended in a draw.

5. **Belgium's Rik Coppens became the first player to do what in 1957?**
   a) Score for three different national teams (France, Netherlands, Belgium)
   b) Score with a two-touch penalty
   c) Play international football across four decades
   d) Captain a national team against a team captained by his brother

6. **Which German star is nicknamed Donkey after he set up an animal charity and had a donkey named after him?**
   a) Florian Wirtz
   b) Jamal Musiala
   c) Kai Havertz
   d) Brajan Gruda

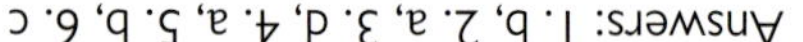
Answers: 1. b, 2. a, 3. d, 4. a, 5. b, 6. c

JULY
15

JULY BIRTHDAYS

JUL

8

SON HEUNG-MIN

South Korean who won nine Asian Player of the Year awards, and the Puskás Award for 2020's best goal

JUL

5

MEGAN RAPINOE

Won the 2015 and 2019 World Cups with USA women while campaigning for social justice

JUL

10

ADA HEGERBERG

Norwegian who won six Champions League finals with Olympique Lyonnais Féminin

JUL

13

LAMINE YAMAL

Spain's youngest player and scorer, netting on his debut aged sixteen

JUL

12

VINICIUS JR

Brazil forward, scored in Real Madrid's 2024 Champions League final win

JUL
16
GARETH BALE
Wales winger who won five Champions League titles with Real Madrid

JUL
21
BRANDI CHASTAIN
Scored USA's winning penalty in the 1999 World Cup final – with her weaker foot

JUL
21
ERLING HAALAND
Norwegian who scored a record 50 Premier League goals in just 48 games for Manchester City

JUL
21
ENDRICK
Brazil's youngest-ever goalscorer aged sixteen

JUL
28
HARRY KANE
England men's all-time leading goalscorer

JUL
26
VICKY LÓPEZ
Spain forward who won back-to-back Women's Champions League titles with Barcelona

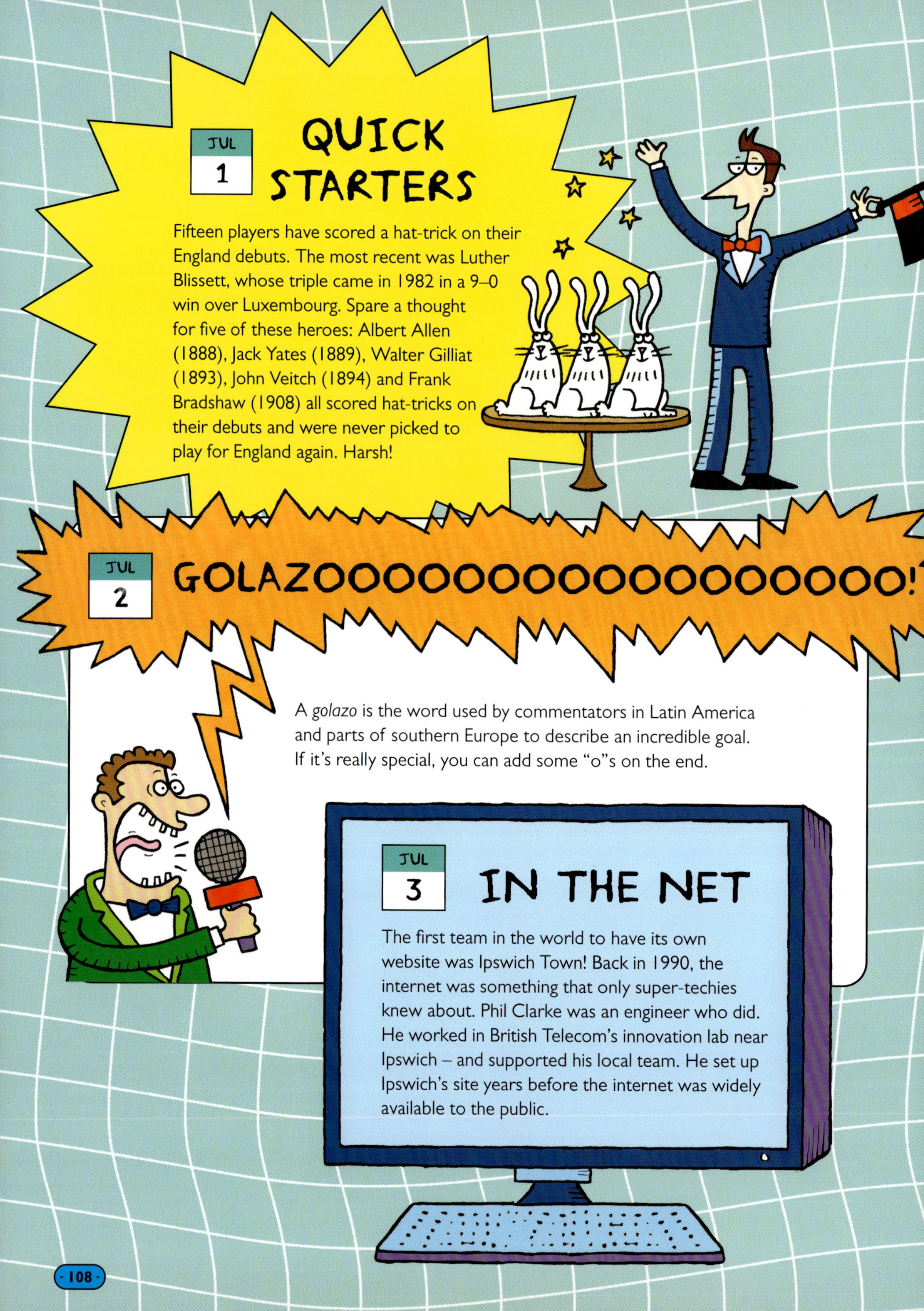

JUL 1 QUICK STARTERS

Fifteen players have scored a hat-trick on their England debuts. The most recent was Luther Blissett, whose triple came in 1982 in a 9–0 win over Luxembourg. Spare a thought for five of these heroes: Albert Allen (1888), Jack Yates (1889), Walter Gilliat (1893), John Veitch (1894) and Frank Bradshaw (1908) all scored hat-tricks on their debuts and were never picked to play for England again. Harsh!

JUL 2 GOLAZOOOOOOOOOOOOOOOOOOOO!

A *golazo* is the word used by commentators in Latin America and parts of southern Europe to describe an incredible goal. If it's really special, you can add some "o"s on the end.

JUL 3 IN THE NET

The first team in the world to have its own website was Ipswich Town! Back in 1990, the internet was something that only super-techies knew about. Phil Clarke was an engineer who did. He worked in British Telecom's innovation lab near Ipswich – and supported his local team. He set up Ipswich's site years before the internet was widely available to the public.

JUL 4

TICK TOCK

The Premier League gives every referee a special watch for matches, with a four-digit timer in the middle that counts down each half from 45:00. The six-digit number below the timer shows the time of the day. The watch vibrates at the end of each half to alert the referee.

JUL 5

THREE AND OUT

Only a handful of players have ever taken three penalties in the same game. So spare a thought for forward Martín Palermo: he is the first player to miss three penalties in the same game. He was playing for Argentina against Colombia in 1998, and his first two kicks were saved; the third hit the crossbar. While Palermo cried in the dressing room after the game, his former team-mate Diego Maradona praised him, saying that the only player who could miss three penalties in one game was the one brave enough to take all three!

JUL 6

GOAL RUSH

The highest-scoring match in European Championship history was the first one ever played: France 4 – Yugoslavia 5 in 1960. Since then, and up to and including Euro 2024, there have been 387 other matches – although none as dramatic as that first one!

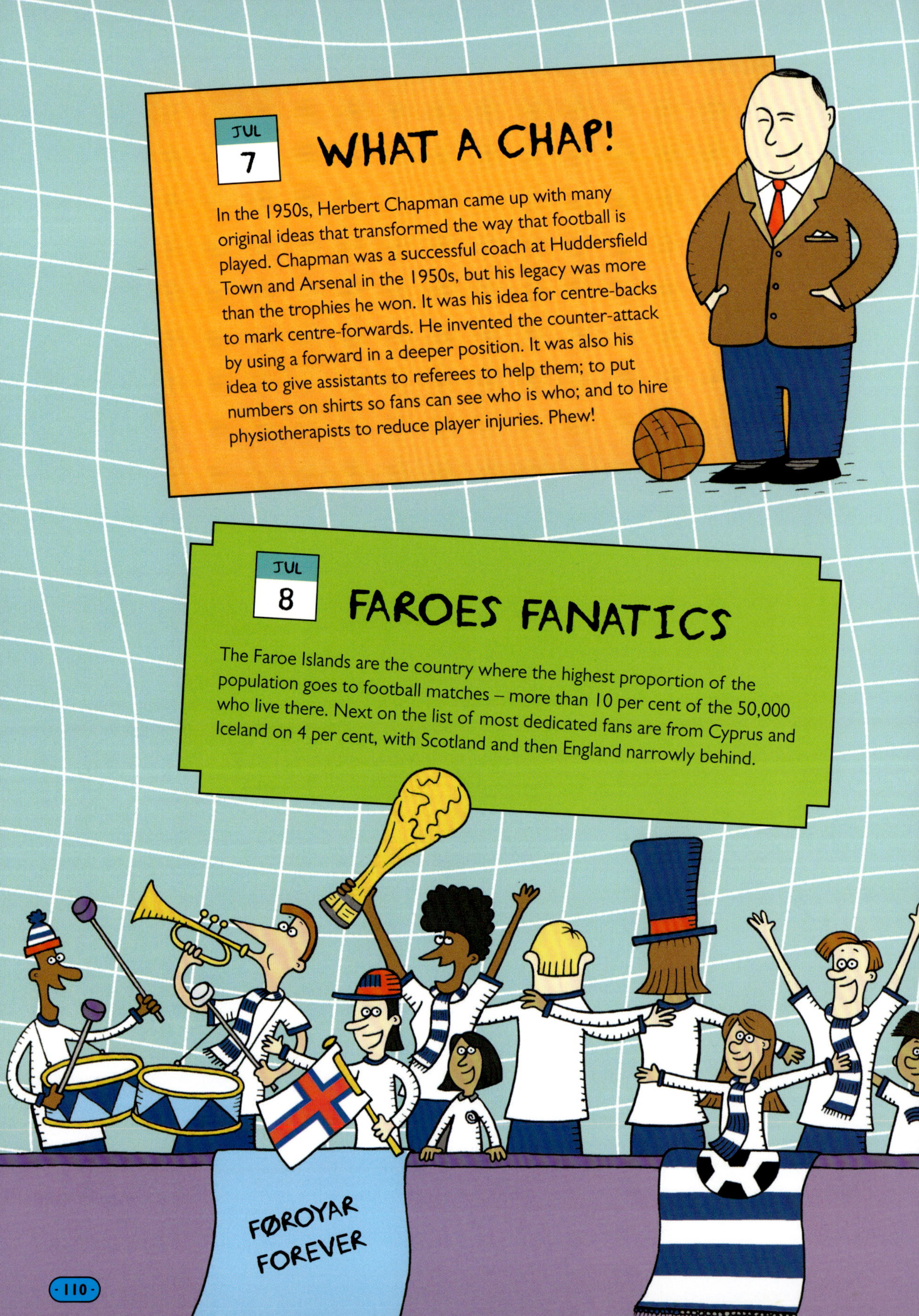

JUL 7

WHAT A CHAP!

In the 1950s, Herbert Chapman came up with many original ideas that transformed the way that football is played. Chapman was a successful coach at Huddersfield Town and Arsenal in the 1950s, but his legacy was more than the trophies he won. It was his idea for centre-backs to mark centre-forwards. He invented the counter-attack by using a forward in a deeper position. It was also his idea to give assistants to referees to help them; to put numbers on shirts so fans can see who is who; and to hire physiotherapists to reduce player injuries. Phew!

JUL 8

FAROES FANATICS

The Faroe Islands are the country where the highest proportion of the population goes to football matches – more than 10 per cent of the 50,000 who live there. Next on the list of most dedicated fans are from Cyprus and Iceland on 4 per cent, with Scotland and then England narrowly behind.

JUL 9

ALFREDO THE GREAT

Real Madrid centre-forward Alfredo di Stéfano scored in each of the first five finals of the European Cup (forerunner to the Champions League) between 1956 and 1960, culminating in his three goals in the 1960 final, a 7–3 win over Eintracht Frankfurt. Di Stéfano also represented three countries – Argentina, Colombia and Spain.

JUL 10

AFRICAN GOLD

Kenya's McDonald Mariga holds the record for a Champions League-winning player to come from the lowest-ranked international team. Mariga was part of the Internazionale squad that won the 2010 European crown, when Kenya was only ranked 113th in the world.

JUL 11

RAMPANT RAFA

Spanish coach Rafa Benítez was in charge of the two teams responsible for the biggest wins in Champions League history: Liverpool beating Beşiktaş 8–0 in 2007, and Real Madrid beating Malmo 8–0 in 2015.

EUROPEAN CUP

JUL 12

HAT-TRICK TRIO

Only three players have ever scored a hat-trick in a World Cup final. All hail this triple-threat trio!

Geoff Hurst England	1966	England 4 West Germany 2
Carli Lloyd USA	2015	USA 5 Japan 2
Kylian Mbappé France	2022	France 3 Argentina 3*

*Argentina won on penalties.

JUL 13

BANG ON THE HEAD

Christoph Kramer was in the Germany team that won the 2014 World Cup final – but he does not remember it. Kramer took a bang to the head in the first half and sustained a concussion, a brain injury that caused him short-term memory loss. Kramer was confused: he asked the referee if the game really was the World Cup final, and tried to remove captain Philipp Lahm's armband. Kramer was subbed off and later made a full recovery.

JUL 14

BELLES ON THE BOX

The biggest TV audience for a football game in the USA – for both men's and women's – was the 2015 Women's World Cup final, when 25 million people watched USA beat China 5–2. What a change from the first Women's World Cup, in 1991, when USA, captained by April Heinrichs, also beat Norway 2–1 in the final – but the match was not broadcast by any US TV channel.

JUL 15 HEROIC HECTOR

One of the heroes of the Uruguay side that won the first-ever World Cup in 1930 played with only half of his right arm. Hector Castro lost his right forearm in an accident involving an electric saw aged thirteen. He went on to become a fearsome striker, scoring Uruguay's first World Cup goal in their opening 1–0 win against Peru as well as the final goal in Uruguay's 4–2 win over Argentina to win the trophy.

JUL 16 RONALDO

Brazilian striker Ronaldo was the world's best player when a horrific knee injury in 1999 almost ended his career. He did not play for nearly two years, but eventually recovered. He made a stunning comeback in the 2002 World Cup, where he scored eight goals (including two in the final) to help Brazil lift the trophy.

JUL 17 HOMARE SAWA

Captain of the Japan women's team that surprisingly beat USA in the 2011 Women's World Cup final, Sawa won the Golden Boot for tournament top scorer. She remains Japan's most capped player (205 appearances) and all-time leading scorer with 83 goals.

JUL 18 HERO PICKLES

An unlikely hero of England's only World Cup success in 1966 was a dog called Pickles. He found the Jules Rimet trophy after it had been stolen just before the tournament. Pickles sniffed it out hidden under a bush in South London during a Sunday walk. His owner, Dave Corbett, took it to the nearest police station. Pickles was then invited to the England team's celebratory dinner, where he weed in the lift and was shown to all the fans by England captain, Bobby Moore.

JUL 19

SHIN STORY

Jack Grealish wears small shin-guards because he finds them more comfortable. He keeps his socks rolled down for superstitious reasons: he once played well in socks he had shrunk in the wash – so he kept them like that. While referees are responsible for checking that every outfield player is wearing shin-guards, they do not check their size and material – it's up to the players to give themselves reasonable protection.

JUL 20

RECORD RIVALS

The first international match played outside of the UK was when Argentina beat Uruguay 6–0 in 1902. Since then, the two countries have enjoyed a close rivalry, with Uruguay getting revenge by beating Argentina 4–2 in the first-ever World Cup final in 1930. The two countries hold the record for the most often played international football fixture, with over 200 matches behind them. Frenemies!

JUL 21

ERLING GOAL-LAND

Erling Haaland is a goalscoring machine! He scored his first 50 Premier League goals in only 48 games, faster than anyone else. He scored his first 40 Champions League goals in only 35 games, faster than anyone else. He scored his first 100 goals for Manchester City in 105 games. And he broke Norway's all-time goalscoring record in 2024 when he scored goal number 34 after just 36 games. The previous record, set by Jørgen "Lightning" Juve, had stood for 90 years!

JUL 22

SUPERHERO STRIKERS

Two players share their names with superhero characters. Brazil striker Givanildo Vieira de Sousa was nicknamed Hulk because he looked like the actor who played the role of main character Bruce Banner in *The Incredible Hulk*. He even had Hulk as the name on the back of his Brazil shirt, which he wore 49 times. Oliver Antman is a winger who made his Finland debut in 2022. Hulk and Antman – there's a double act that would be dramatic!

ESTADIO MARIA

Uruguayan club Danubio was founded by two Bulgarian-born brothers in 1932 and named after the Danube River, Europe's second-longest river, which runs through Bulgaria. When their stadium was renamed in 1998, members voted for it to be named after the person who suggested the club's name, and was also the mother of those two brothers. Danubio now plays at the Jardines del Hipodromo María Mincheff de Lazaroff Stadium.

JUL
24

BLOOD ON THE PITCH

Chile goalkeeper Roberto Rojas was banned from football for life in 1989 – and his country kicked out of the World Cup – after pretending that he had been injured by a firecracker that had been thrown onto the pitch during a World Cup qualifying game. He dived into the smoke of the firecracker and emerged bleeding, but it was later discovered that he had cut himself using a razor-blade hidden in his gloves so he could get the match abandoned.

JUL 25

FAB FIFTEEN

The first player under sixteen to play in the Premier League was English midfielder Ethan Nwaneri, who was aged fifteen years and 181 days when he played for Arsenal against Brentford in 2022.

JUL 26

SWEET SIXTEEN

Spain forward Vicky López is the youngest player to play for Barcelona in the Champions League, the youngest player to play in the Barcelona stadium, Camp Nou, and the youngest player to score against their fierce rivals, Real Madrid. And she did it all before she turned seventeen! Vicky was actually born in Madrid, so scoring Barcelona's final goal in a 5–0 win was a bit awkward!

JUL 27

A FOOTBALLING SPY

Cândido de Oliveira was Portugal's captain for their first-ever match in 1921, and he went on to coach the team at the 1928 Olympic Games. During the Second World War, he worked in the Portuguese post office and became a British spy, intercepting letters from Nazi Germany. He was caught by a secret police officer, his former goalkeeper, Antonio Roquette, and spent two years in a prison camp before founding Portugal's biggest sports newspaper, *A Bola*.

JUL 28

POWER HIT

England striker Chloe Kelly struck a penalty in the 2023 Women's World Cup that was clocked at 110 km/h – faster than the fastest shot in the Premier League that season! Kelly's power hit came during England's penalty shoot-out win over Nigeria and was a combination of strength, balance, timing and body rotation. "I was trying to be bold," said Kelly.

JUL 29

JAMES AND JAMES

Reece and Lauren James are the first brother and sister combination to play for England. Their dad, Nigel, was a football coach who trained them both in his back garden. Reece made his England debut in 2020 while Lauren followed up with her debut in 2022.

JUL 30

GAME-CHANGERS

Today's version of football is very different from how it looked when it was first established in the 19th century. Here are some of the most important inventions that have changed the game:

Innovation	Date	Purpose
Goal nets	1891	Made it clear a goal had been scored
Substitutes	1965	Allowed players to be replaced mid-game
Penalty shoot-out	1970	Decided the winner in a drawn match
Red cards	1970	Showed who had been sent off
VAR	2016	Allowed tough referee decisions to be checked using video

JUL 31

FOUR SCORES!

Japanese people have the longest life expectancy in the world, at 84.3 years: this helps to explain why the country has a league for players who are over 80. The Over-80 league features three teams – Red Star, White Bears and Blue Hawaii. The matches are eleven-a-side, and made up of two fifteen-minute halves. Teams can have unlimited substitutes and – for obvious reasons – sliding tackles are banned!

JULY QUIZ

1. What was special about the first-ever match in the European Championship, between France and Yugoslavia in 1960?

a) It remains the highest-scoring match in the tournament's history.
b) Both teams went on to win the first two editions of the tournament.
c) It was the only 0–0 ever played in the tournament.
d) The first half was played in France, and the second half in Yugoslavia.

2. Place, in order of which came first, the following football inventions:

a) Goal nets
b) VAR
c) Red cards
d) Substitutes

3. What was special about Hector Castro, who scored for Uruguay in their 1930 World Cup final win over Argentina?

a) He was the fastest man in the world.
b) He was the goalkeeper.
c) He lost his right forearm in an accident when he was thirteen.
d) He was born in Argentina.

4. Complete the following sentence correctly: The Faroe Islands is the country where ...

a) ... there is a league for players aged over 80.
b) ... the national team captain addresses the nation on Christmas Day.
c) ... the highest proportion of its population goes to football matches.
d) ... league matches last 80 minutes because it gets dark so early.

5. What is the most-played international match in history, excluding teams from the UK?

a) France vs Belgium
b) USA vs Mexico
c) Ghana vs Nigeria
d) Argentina vs Uruguay

6. What is Argentina striker Martín Palermo's penalty claim to fame?

a) He taught Diego Maradona how to take penalties.
b) He missed three penalties in one match for Argentina.
c) He broke the crossbar and caused a World Cup match to be abandoned.
d) He was the only outfield player to save a penalty in a shoot-out.

Answers: 1. a, 2. a), d), c), b), 3. c, 4. c, 5. d, 6. b

AUGUST

AUGUST BIRTHDAYS
AUG
5
GAVI
Won the 2022 Kopa Trophy for best U-21 player, played for Spain at the World Cup aged eighteen
AUG
7
LAUREN HEMP
England Euro 2022 winner, scored in the World Cup quarters and semis to reach 2023 final
AUG
7
MATTY CASH
Poland defender who played in the Premier League and 2022 World Cup
AUG
10
SOPHIA SMITH
Prolific USA striker, missed shoot-out penalty in 2023 World Cup defeat
AUG
10
BERNARDO SILVA
Portugal midfielder, league winner with Benfica, Monaco and Manchester City

AUG
17
EDERSON
Brazil goalkeeper and multiple Premier League champion
AUG
21
MILLIE BRIGHT
Six-time WSL winner with Chelsea and Euro 2022 winner
I like to eat bangers - and score them too!
AUG
22
LAUTARO MARTÍNEZ
Argentina's 2022 World Cup winner
AUG
21
ROBERT LEWANDOWSKI
Poland's all-time leading goalscorer, title winner in Poland, Germany and Spain
AUG
24
GONÇALO INÁCIO
Portugal defender who burst out at Euro 2024
AUG
30
YVES BISSOUMA
Mali midfielder who played in the Premier League

AUG 1

QUICK JOB

In 2007, Leroy Rosenior took the job as head coach of Torquay United. He was sacked ten minutes later, as a new owner came in just after his appointment and wasted no time in making a change.

AUG 2

SHOOTING STARS

Players at the highest level are getting better at scoring goals: the conversion rate of all shots on goal at the 1986 World Cup was around 8 per cent, which by the 2022 World Cup had increased to nearly 12 per cent. The number of shots per game has decreased (29 to 22), which suggests players are now waiting to get into better scoring positions before taking a shot on goal.

AUG 3

MARY'S ACTS NOW IN WAX

In 2023, Mary Earps played in the Women's World Cup final for England, won FIFA's Golden Glove and The Best award for best goalkeeper. As a tribute to her success, fans elected her Sports Personality of the Year and voted for her to become the first female footballer to have her likeness recreated at the Madame Tussauds London waxwork museum.

AUG 4

FAN TO THE RESCUE

After Uruguay side Peñarol brought the wrong-coloured goalkeeper jersey to an away match at rivals Progreso in 2018, they came up with a unique solution. They found a fan in the crowd who was wearing the correct goalkeeper top and asked to borrow his shirt. In return, they loaned him a club jacket to keep him warm. The top did the job: Peñarol won the game 1–0!

FLY BY

North Korea's national team is nicknamed The Chollima, which is a mythical winged horse that flies at supersonic speeds and can never be mounted by a mortal.

HOME-GROWN

More than one hundred men's teams and more than thirty women's teams playing at the World Cup have been led by foreign coaches – but none has ever won the trophy. A foreign coach has only reached the final twice: England's George Raynor, coach of Sweden, in 1958 and Austria's Ernst Happel, who coached the Netherlands in 1978. The two teams with the most World Cup final appearances, Brazil and Germany, have always had native coaches.

In August, around most of Europe, the football season starts for the national league competitions. Join us for a whistle-stop tour around Europe as we meet some interesting fans – and the GOAT goat!

AUG 7 WHAT NO KEEPER?

French club Bordeaux lined up in 1982 for a league match against Nantes without a goalkeeper! It was in protest at their goalkeeper being banned for kicking an assistant referee. Bordeaux's shortest midfielder, Alain Giresse, wore the goalkeeper jersey, but still played in midfield. Nantes won the game 6–0 – not bad, really!

AUG 8 IMPROVES WITH AGE

Portugal forward Cristiano Ronaldo began his career at Sporting Lisbon. In his first season as a pro, he only scored three goals in 25 games. But Ronaldo improved as he got older, becoming the all-time top scorer for Real Madrid and Portugal. He has also scored more international goals than anyone else in men's football.

FRANCE

AUG 9 MAD-JESTY!

"*Real*" in Spanish means royal. It has been used in the club name Real Madrid ever since 1920, when King Alfonso XIII of Spain gave Madrid Club de Futbol permission to use the title. In the 1950s, Real Madrid won the first five editions of the European Cup (the forerunner to the Champions League), and they became footballing royalty, too!

AUG 10 HOOF IT, HENNES

German club Cologne have a mascot called Hennes the Goat, who comes to all home matches. The tradition started in 1950, when a circus owner gave a billy goat to the club as a lucky charm. They named him after Hennes Weisweiler, who was Cologne coach at the time. Goats have a lifespan of about fifteen years, and the current Hennes is their ninth, known as Hennes IX.

AUG 11 DOING THE POZNAŃ

Fans of Polish club Lech Poznań celebrate goals by turning their back on the pitch, putting their arms around each other's shoulders and bouncing up and down. When Poznań faced Manchester City in a European match in 2010, the City fans loved it and adopted the same celebration. It's now known as "doing the Poznań".

AUG 12 MISTER MEN

Italian players call their coaches "Mister", a term that dates back to the early 1900s, when English coaches travelled to Europe to educate other teams. The coach who won Italy's first-ever league title in 1924, with Genoa, was an Englishman called William Garbutt. What a master Mister!

ITALY

AUGUST

AUG 13

REVOLTING ORANGE

The Netherlands flag is red, white and blue but their national team football kit is orange. This links to William of Orange, the leader of a Dutch revolt against Spanish rule in 1568, which eventually led to the Netherlands' independence in 1648. William of Orange remains a Dutch national hero, even though the Orange in his name actually refers to his birthplace … in France!

AUG 14

LONG PENS

The longest penalty shoot-out in any European competition took place in the 2024 Europa League qualifying tie between Dutch team Ajax and Greek side Panathinaikos. A total of 34 penalties were taken. Ajax missed four penalties but eventually won the shoot-out 13–12.

AUG 15

OH MUUUUUM!

The first parent-child combination to play football together for their country was mother-and-daughter pair Bára Skaale Klakstein and Eydvør Klakstein of the Faroe Islands in 2012. Mother Bára started the 6–0 win over Luxembourg and, after an hour, her daughter Eydvør came on to play alongside her.

VADUZ IT AGAIN

Liechtenstein is the only UEFA member country without a football league. Instead, its biggest club, Vaduz, plays league football in Switzerland. Vaduz regularly qualifies for European competitions by winning the Liechtenstein Cup competition (played in the country without a league), which it has done a world-record 50 times.

AUG 17

COR SKILLS

Haiti midfielder Melchie Dumornay, known as Corventina, was voted best player at the CONCACAF Under-17 championship – aged only fourteen. Since then, Corventina – a nickname given by her brother Corvington – has just got better and better. She helped Haiti qualify for its first-ever Women's World Cup in 2023. Then she won goal of the tournament in the 2024 Women's Champions League and was named UEFA's young player of the 2024 season after moving to Olympique Lyonnais Féminin. Haiti, in the Caribbean, is one of the poorest countries in the world, which makes Corventina's achievement even more amazing!

AUG 18

SHARING IS CARING

These teams are local rivals and also share the same stadium:

Teams	Stadium	Location
Beitar Jerusalem, Hapoel Jersualem	Teddy	Jerusalem, Israel
Djurgårdens, Hammarby	3Arena	Stockholm, Sweden
Esteghlal, Persepolis	Azadi	Tehran, Iran
Flamengo, Fluminense	Maracanã	Rio, Brazil
Internazionale, AC Milan	San Siro	Milan, Italy
Lazio, Roma	Stadio Olimpico	Rome, Italy
Tokyo FC, Tokyo Verdy	Ajinomoto	Tokyo, Japan

AUG 19

LEFT BEHIND

About ten per cent of people are left-handed, while twelve per cent are left-footed. The second figure is higher among professional footballers at around twenty per cent. Some of the best players ever were left-footed – maybe because right-footers find it harder to play against them! Famous left-footers include Johan Cruyff, Diego Maradona, Ferenc Puskás and Lionel Messi.

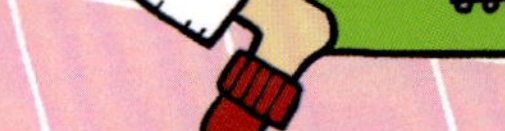

AUG 20 DINO POWER

Arsenal mascot, Gunnersaurus Rex, was invented by an eleven-year-old called Peter Lovell, who, in 1993, won a competition run by the club to design the mascot. Gunnersaurus made his first appearance in a home match against Manchester City on this day in 1994 – which Arsenal won 3–0!

AUG 21 HIDDEN CUP

The Jules Rimet trophy, awarded for winning the World Cup, spent the Second World War under a bed. At the beginning of the war, the trophy, which had been won by Italy in 1938, was kept in a bank in Rome. FIFA's Italian vice-president, Dr Ottorino Barassi, then took it home to stop the Nazis stealing it. He hid it in a shoebox under his bed!

AUG 22

OLD NAME NEW NAME

Some English and Welsh clubs changed their names before taking on their current team names. Here are a few.

Original name	Founded	Changed to	In
Christchurch Rangers	1882	Queens Park Rangers	1886
Black Arabs	1883	Bristol Rovers	1898
Singers	1883	Coventry City	1898
Ardwick	1887	Manchester City	1894
Headington	1893	Oxford United	1960
Riverside	1899	Cardiff City	1908

AUG 23

POKE EYE MAN

The shortest substitute appearance belongs to Swedish team Degerfors defender Mattias Özgün. He lasted a few seconds on the pitch of a 2019 game before going off injured, after the team-mate he replaced, Axel Lindahl, accidentally poked him in the eye during an attempted high-five. Ouch!

AUG 24

NEVER GIVE UP

Bayer Leverkusen became the first German team to win the Bundesliga title after going the whole season undefeated in 2024. Their achievement was even more remarkable because it was their first-ever title. They also won the German Cup, completing a run of 51 consecutive matches without defeat. In 2002, they were set to win everything, but missed out on the title by one point, and lost the German Cup and Champions League final. That earned them the nickname "Bayer Neverkusen". Not any more – now they are Winnerkusen!

AUG 25

HUNGARY FOR RECORDS

The best football team you've never heard of might be the Hungary national team of the 1950s. This "Golden Team" went unbeaten for over four years, scored at least one goal in 73 consecutive games and averaged over five goals per game in the 1954 World Cup finals. They were the first non-British side to beat England at home (6–3 in 1953) and handed England their heaviest defeat (7–1, a record that still stands). But, from 2–0 up, they lost the 1954 World Cup final to West Germany, who they had beaten 8–3 a few weeks earlier. Had they won the World Cup, we'd still be talking about them as one of the greatest teams of all time!

*Turkish for street

AUG 26

REF SEES RED

In a Turkish league match in 2016, defender Salih Dursun thought he would relax the atmosphere after referee Deniz Ateş Bitnel had sent off his Trabzonspor team-mate and then dropped his red card. As Dursun handed the card back to the official, he jokingly waved it in his direction – and got sent off, too! Fans were so angry with the referee (he dismissed four Trabzonspor players in the game) that Dursun became a hero. He even had a street named in his honour.

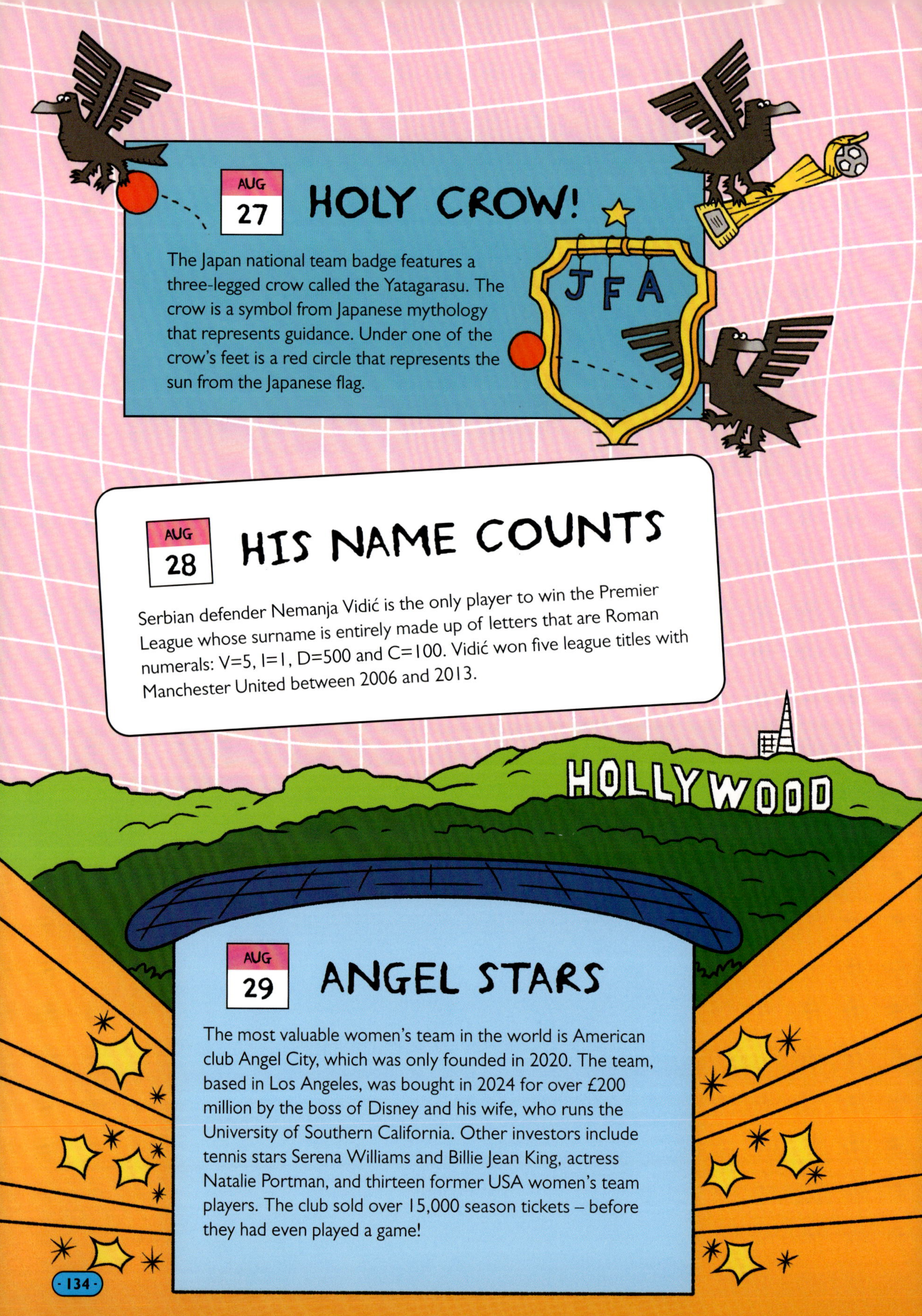

AUG 27

HOLY CROW!

The Japan national team badge features a three-legged crow called the Yatagarasu. The crow is a symbol from Japanese mythology that represents guidance. Under one of the crow's feet is a red circle that represents the sun from the Japanese flag.

AUG 28

HIS NAME COUNTS

Serbian defender Nemanja Vidić is the only player to win the Premier League whose surname is entirely made up of letters that are Roman numerals: V=5, I=1, D=500 and C=100. Vidić won five league titles with Manchester United between 2006 and 2013.

AUG 29

ANGEL STARS

The most valuable women's team in the world is American club Angel City, which was only founded in 2020. The team, based in Los Angeles, was bought in 2024 for over £200 million by the boss of Disney and his wife, who runs the University of Southern California. Other investors include tennis stars Serena Williams and Billie Jean King, actress Natalie Portman, and thirteen former USA women's team players. The club sold over 15,000 season tickets – before they had even played a game!

AUG 30

BIRTHDAY HATS

Two players have scored Premier League hat-tricks on their birthdays: Jimmy Floyd Hasselbaink for Chelsea in 2004, when he turned 32, and Carlos Tevez for Manchester City against West Bromwich Albion, aged 27. Four players – Gerry Taggart (aged 27, Bolton), Les Ferdinand (27, QPR), Dwight Gayle (26, Crystal Palace) and Wilfred Ndidi (21, Leicester) – were sent off on their birthday. That's the wrong kind of card to get!

AUG 31

FOR MY NEXT TRICK

There is more than one definition of a perfect hat-trick. In Germany, a perfect hat-trick is when a player scores three goals – with no other goals between them – in the same half. In England, a perfect hat-trick is when the player scores with left foot, then right foot, then a header, in that order. Congratulations, then, to Erling Haaland, who in August 2022 scored a *perfect* perfect hat-trick for Manchester City with three uninterrupted first-half goals, using his body parts in the right order (left, right, head), in a 6–0 win over Nottingham Forest. Hats off!

AUGUST QUIZ

1. **Which is the only national association in UEFA without its own league?**
   a) Liechtenstein
   b) San Marino
   c) Gibraltar
   d) Wales

2. **What World Cup fact links English coach George Raynor with Austrian coach Ernst Happel?**
   a) They coached England and West Germany, respectively, in their 1966 World Cup final.
   b) They were winning coaches of the first-ever World Cup matches played in 1930.
   c) They are the first former World Cup players who went on to coach their national teams at a World Cup.
   d) They are the only two foreign coaches to lead teams to a World Cup final (Sweden 1958 and Netherlands 1978).

3. **How did French club Bordeaux protest at a referee's decision to ban their goalkeeper for a match in 1982?**
   a) They picked three reserve goalkeepers, all of who stayed in goal (with only one handling the ball), during a 0–0 draw.
   b) They lined up without a goalkeeper and lost 6–0.
   c) The club owner played in goal and they lost 3–1.
   d) The coach played in goal and they won 4–3.

4. **Dating back from a tradition that started in 1950, German club Cologne has a goat mascot at every home game. Why is the goat called Hennes?**
   a) Named after the Cologne coach in charge at the time, Hennes Weisweller
   b) Named after the circus owner who donated the goat, Hennes Althoff
   c) Named after Cologne's longest-serving player, Hennes Schäfer
   d) All goats in Germany are called Hennes.

5. **Can you match these English teams to their original names when they were first set up?**

a) Manchester City	1. Headington
b) Coventry City	2. Christchurch Rangers
c) Queens Park Rangers	3. Ardwick
d) Oxford United	4. Singers

6. **How do fans of Polish club Lech Poznań celebrate goals?**
   a) Sing the Polish national anthem
   b) Take off their shirts and wave them around their heads
   c) Suck their thumbs
   d) Turn their backs to the pitch and bounce up and down

Answers: 1. a, 2 d, 3. b, 4. a, 5. a) 3, b) 4, c) 2, d) 1, 6. d

SEPTEMBER
NOBEL PRIZE

SEPTEMBER BIRTHDAYS

SEP
13
PEDRO PORRO
All-action Spain wing-back
SEP
19
KIERAN TRIPPIER
Scored for England in the 2018 World Cup semi-final
SEP
22
THIAGO SILVA
Brazil captain, played in four World Cups
SEP
27
CLAUDIO GENTILE
Tough tackler, won the 1982 World Cup with Italy
SEP
29
LAUREN JAMES
Part of England team that reached the 2023 Women's World Cup final
SEP
30
OLIVIER GIROUD
France's all-time leading scorer, title winner in France and Italy
SEPTEMBER

SEP 1 MADE IN WALES

Gareth Bale broke the world transfer record in 2013 when he moved from Tottenham Hotspur to Real Madrid for £85 million. He was the second Welshman to break the record, after striker Trevor Ford moved from Aston Villa to Sunderland for £30,000 in 1950. Ford has another claim to fame: he was fielding for Welsh cricket side Glamorgan in 1968 when West Indian star Garfield Sobers hit six sixes in one over against them!

SEP 2 WINNING WENDIE

Wendie Renard holds the record for most consecutive league titles while playing in a major European league. The French defender spent her whole career at Olympique Lyonnais Féminin and won fourteen consecutive Première Ligue women's titles from 2007 to 2020.

SEP 3 FAIR AND SQUARE

Fans of French club Saint-Étienne remain convinced that they would have won the 1976 European Cup final – if only the posts had been rounded, and not with a sharp edge! Saint-Étienne lost 1–0 to Bayern Munich but when the score was goalless they twice hit the crossbar, which in those days had a sharp edge. Experts have since shown that the ball would have rebounded down and over the line if the crossbar was rounded like a pole, as they are now. The square goalposts, known in France as *les poteaux carrés*, now take pride of place in Saint-Étienne's club museum.

SEP 4

WHAT'S IN A NAME?

Club name	Country	Why?
Always Ready	Bolivia	Named after the Scouts' motto
Hearts of Oak	Ghana	Refers to the strongest part of an oak tree
Kaizer Chiefs	South Africa	Founded by ex-Atlanta Chiefs striker Kaizer Motaung
Kashima Antlers	Japan	Kashima translates as "Deer Island"
Queen of the South	Scotland	Nickname given in 1857 to the club's town, Dumfries

SEP 5

RIDE RELIEF!

Anyone mowing the grass of a football pitch must be glad of ride-on lawnmowers. Mowing one football pitch takes around twelve kilometres of walking power – and in the summer, some pitches are mown two, or even three, times a day!

SEP 6 — WHO'S THE REFEREE IN DISGUISE?

Livion Bonelli was an Argentinian referee with a clever way of escaping from angry fans after a game. Bonelli refereed matches in disguise, wearing a wig and a false beard, which he could whip off after a game if he thought fans were unhappy with his decisions. It was reported that his disguise twice helped him to avoid trouble.

SEP 7 — FLIPPY DISC

Most referees use a normal coin to toss up between the captains to choose the ends before a match. But in the Champions League, UEFA gives its referees a disc with blue on one side and red on the other.

SEP 8 — FEE FACTS

Top-flight referees in Spain are the best paid on average, according to a study carried out in 2024. Premier League referees are paid on a scale depending on their experience and seniority. Every referee also gets a separate fee per match they are in charge of. In Germany, where the salaries are lowest, the match fees are highest, at almost £5,000 per game. In the Premier League, the match fee is just over £1,000.

Average salary of football referees (not including match fees)

SEP 9 PANENKA PENALTY

Antonín Panenka scored one of the most famous penalties in history when his slow chipped dink down the middle of the goal won Euro 1976 for Czechoslovakia against West Germany. Panenka had practised the penalty for two years before taking it, winning lots of chocolate in bets on the outcome from his goalkeeper team-mate Zdeněk Hruška. The penalty became so popular that any chipped penalty down the middle of the goal is now called "a Panenka".

SEP 10 LEFT AND RIGHT

Germany defender Andreas Brehme scored a penalty in the 1986 World Cup with his left foot, and in the 1990 World Cup final with his right foot. He remains the only player to score penalties with both feet in the World Cup. In the Premier League, England forward Bobby Zamora and Nigeria striker Obafemi Martins have scored penalties with both feet. Spain midfielder Santi Cazorla went one better: he scored "Panenka" penalties with his left and right foot.

SEP 11

THE MAN THAT MAKES THE RULES

The most senior referee in the world used to be a geography teacher. David Elleray taught at a boys' secondary school as well as being a referee. At the time, referees were amateurs. Now he is the technical director for the International Football Association Board (IFAB), the organization that updates the Laws of the Game. Elleray says his previous career as a teacher helps him today – telling people what to do and handing out punishments!

SEP 12

WIEGMAN WISDOM

Dutch coach Sarina Wiegman, who was in charge of the England women's team when they won Euro 2022, credits her communication, organization and leadership skills to taking a job early in her career as a PE teacher. She was also the first Dutch player to win 100 appearances for her country.

SEP 13

TRACKSUIT TEACHER

Former England coach Roy Hodgson began his career as an English teacher in South London – before swapping books for balls. Hodgson ended up learning seven languages as he coached thirteen clubs in six different countries. He also guided the national teams of Switzerland, the United Arab Emirates and Finland before taking the England job.

SEP 14

SCHOOL CAPTAINS

The only school to produce two record-breaking England captains is Chingford Foundation School in Essex. David Beckham, who played more England matches while playing for non-English teams than anyone else, was a pupil at the secondary school, and twenty years later Harry Kane, England's all-time leading scorer, also attended. Kane later said Beckham's career, from the same school roots, inspired him.

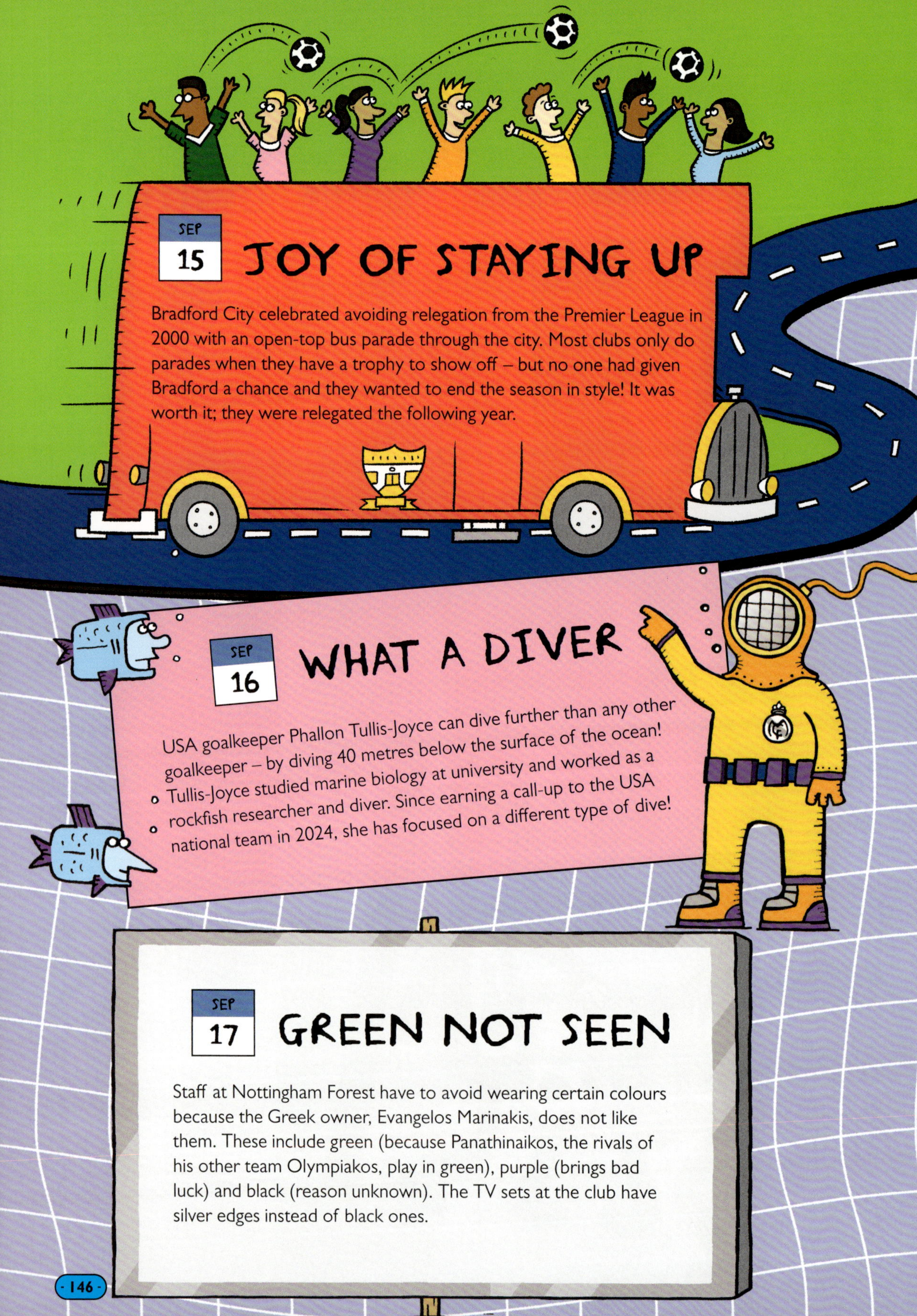

SEP 15

JOY OF STAYING UP

Bradford City celebrated avoiding relegation from the Premier League in 2000 with an open-top bus parade through the city. Most clubs only do parades when they have a trophy to show off – but no one had given Bradford a chance and they wanted to end the season in style! It was worth it; they were relegated the following year.

SEP 16

WHAT A DIVER

USA goalkeeper Phallon Tullis-Joyce can dive further than any other goalkeeper – by diving 40 metres below the surface of the ocean! Tullis-Joyce studied marine biology at university and worked as a rockfish researcher and diver. Since earning a call-up to the USA national team in 2024, she has focused on a different type of dive!

SEP 17

GREEN NOT SEEN

Staff at Nottingham Forest have to avoid wearing certain colours because the Greek owner, Evangelos Marinakis, does not like them. These include green (because Panathinaikos, the rivals of his other team Olympiakos, play in green), purple (brings bad luck) and black (reason unknown). The TV sets at the club have silver edges instead of black ones.

SEP 18

BRAINY BALLER

The only player to win one of science's most important prizes is Niels Bohr, who won the Nobel Prize in 1922 for his contribution to physics. Bohr played as a goalkeeper for a Danish club called AB, which stands for Akademisk Boldklub. It just so happens that Ben (whose birthday is today) is now a co-owner of this club. He likes to make sure that all the players (and fans) read and learn through football!

SEP 19

YOU'RE FIRED!

Romanian team FCU Craiova have hired Italian coach Nicolò Napoli ten times – and fired him ten times, too! He was first appointed in 2003, and most recently in 2024. He was replaced by Eugen Trică, who himself was appointed for the fifth time. Make up your mind!

SEP 20

KEYS TO SUCCESS

Many players believe that playing the piano can help them relax and stay calm away from the pitch. Piano-playing pros include Dutch defender Nathan Aké, Belgian forward Loïs Openda and Spanish 2023 Women's World Cup winner Mariona Caldentey. "It's a good getaway for mental health," says Premier League winner Aké, who has bought musical instruments for six schools in Manchester. Maybe the players should get together for a concert!

SEP 21

OPEN AFCON

The Africa Cup of Nations (AFCON) is one of the most open tournaments in the world. The 2023 edition had eight different teams in the last eight compared to the 2021 edition, as all of the top-five ranked countries, including champions Senegal, were eliminated. This has never happened before in any major continental tournament!

SEP 22

NOT YOU AGAIN!

The most-played derby match in the world is between Glasgow rivals Celtic and Rangers. The teams have faced each other over 440 times, dating back to 1891. The next most common derby match is also in Scotland, between Edinburgh teams Hibernian and Heart of Midlothian (first game 1875). In mainland Europe, the most frequent derby comes from Austria, where top-flight teams Rapid Vienna and Austria Vienna have been doing battle since 1911.

SEP 23

TWIN PEAKS

Identical twin brothers Hossam and Ibrahim Hassan made a world-record combined total of 311 international appearances for Egypt. Here are some other identical twins who also played for their country.

Surname	First names	Country
Altintop	Hamit, Halil	Turkey
Arveladze	Shota, Archil	Georgia
Berezutski	Vasiliy, Aleksei	Russia
De Boer	Frank, Ronald	Netherlands
Degen	David, Philipp	Switzerland
Holmgaard	Sara, Karen	Denmark
Ravelli	Thomas, Andreas	Sweden
Van de Kerkhof	Willy, René	Netherlands

SEP 24

SOY INVINCIBLE

Spanish midfielder Rodri holds the record for most consecutive matches played for one team without losing, when he went 74 games unbeaten for Manchester City between 2022 and 2024. In that period, he helped the team win two Premier League titles, two FA Cups, one Super Cup, one Club World Cup and the 2023 Champions League final – he even scored the winning goal in the final! No wonder he was awarded the Ballon d'Or in 2024 for the world's best player!

LUTON LEGEND

English midfielder Pelly Ruddock Mpanzu is the first player to progress from the fifth tier to the top tier in the football league pyramid with the same club. Mpanzu joined Luton Town in 2013, when they were in the fifth level, the National League, and helped them win promotion to League Two (2014), to League One (2018), to the Championship (2019) and finally to the Premier League (2023). Ten years, five leagues – one amazing player!

SHAGGY DOG STORY

During the 1962 World Cup quarter-final between Brazil and England, a dog ran onto the pitch. He ran away from Brazil pair Gilmar and Garrincha, and was carried off the pitch by England striker Jimmy Greaves, who approached him on all fours. The dog weed down the front of Greaves's shirt while he was being carried off. A Brazilian magazine took the dog back to Brazil, where he was won in a raffle … by Garrincha!

SEP
27

Historic Trio

Aston Villa, Blackburn and Everton are the only clubs that were founder members of both the Football League in 1888 and the Premier League in 1992.

THREE-SY DOES IT

Colombia's Linda Caicedo is the first player to play in three World Cups within the space of one year. In August 2022, the winger scored two goals as Colombia reached the Under-20 World Cup quarter-finals. A few months later, she helped Colombia reach the Under-17 World Cup final, joint-top scorer with three goals. And in summer 2023, then only eighteen, she starred at the main event: the Women's World Cup, where she won Goal of the Tournament for a stunning strike against Germany. Linda leathered it!

STRONGEST BY NAME

The oldest football club in Bolivia is called "The Strongest". Their founders wanted a name that would last a long time, so originally called the club Strong, before changing to an even stronger name. They are the only team to spend over 100 consecutive years in the top division and in 1930, won the league title without conceding a single goal. Soon after that, the team joined the Bolivian army to defeat Paraguay in a battle over a stretch of land. Strongest on and off the pitch!

SEP
30

ON THE MOVE

Uruguay forward Sebastián Abreu has played for more clubs than any other player: 32 clubs in eleven different countries over a 26-year career. Abreu, an expert in scoring chipped "Panenka" penalties, played for Uruguay in two World Cups and helped them win the 2011 Copa América.

SEPTEMBER QUIZ

1. **How much walking does it take to mow one full-sized football pitch?**
   a) 6 kilometres
   b) 10 kilometres
   c) 12 kilometres
   d) 15 kilometres

2. **Complete the following sentence correctly: French defender Wendie Renard has won ...**
   a) ... the Ballon d'Or three times.
   b) ... the French league title fourteen times running with Olympique Lyonnais Féminin.
   c) ... the Champions League and World Cup in the same year.
   d) ... nothing in her career.

3. **What is the most-played derby match, a game between two local rivals, in the world?**
   a) Rapid Vienna vs Austria Vienna
   b) Arsenal vs Tottenham Hotspur
   c) Celtic vs Rangers
   d) Galatasaray vs Fenerbahçe

4. **What is a "Panenka", named after Czech star Antonín Panenka's winning contribution to the 1976 European Championship final?**
   a) A shot that goes in off the crossbar
   b) A hat-trick of headers
   c) When someone drops a trophy by mistake
   d) A chipped penalty down the middle of the goal

5. **What do former England captain David Beckham and England's leading scorer Harry Kane have in common?**
   a) They went to the same school in Essex.
   b) They were born in the same hospital in London.
   c) They both came through the Arsenal academy.
   d) They are cousins.

6. **German defender Andreas Brehme is the only player to do what in the World Cup?**
   a) Win the trophy with two different countries
   b) Score a penalty with his left foot and his right foot
   c) Score a hat-trick and get sent off in the same game
   d) Play in a match refereed by his dad

Answers: 1. c, 2. b, 3. c, 4. d, 5. a, 6. b

OCTOBER
10
150

OCTOBER BIRTHDAYS

OCT **2** ÁLISSON BECKER

Brazil goalkeeper and Champions League winner with Liverpool

OCT **4** CATARINO MACÁRIO

USA striker won the 2022 Champions League with Olympique Lyonnais Féminin

OCT **14** ALEX SCOTT

England defender, now a TV presenter and sports pundit

OCT **15** DIDIER DESCHAMPS

Won the World Cup with France as captain in 1998 and coach in 2018

OCT **23** PELÉ

Brazil's hero, the only player to win three World Cups

OCT

24 İLKAY GÜNDOĞAN

German midfielder, scored the goal that clinched the 2023 Premier League title

OCT

27 DAYOT UPAMECANO

France defender, reached the 2022 World Cup final

OCT

27 JESS CARTER

Euro 2022 winner with England and five-time Women's Super League champion

OCT

28 LUCY BRONZE

England right-back, Ballon d'Or runner-up and four-time Champions League winner

OCT

30 DIEGO MARADONA

Argentina icon who won the 1986 World Cup

OCT

31 ANSU FATI

Spain forward, youngest player to score in the Champions League at sixteen

KICKS AND KOCS

OCT 1

The English word coach comes from the Hungarian town Kocs, where in the 15th century they designed a type of horse-drawn cart with metal suspension. The word later gained a new meaning as someone who trains athletes, since the coach helps to "transport" the athletes to their sporting goals.

OCT 2

WELCOME TO MALAGA!

Fans of Spanish side Malaga were frustrated that no new players signed in summer 2023. To make their feelings clear, they stood outside the local airport and welcomed random arrivals with cheers and songs as though they had just signed for the team.

OCT 3

BIZARRO

Peruvian striker Claudio Pizarro holds the world record for signing for the same club the most times. Pizarro, who had a spell at Chelsea in 2007, loved playing for German side Werder Bremen – but not as much as they loved signing him! Bremen signed Pizarro on five separate occasions between 2001 and 2018 – a world record.

OCT 4

WELCOME TO FIFA

FIFA is football's world governing body. At the time of writing, it has 211 members, and it regularly receives requests from new countries to join. This century FIFA has welcomed these five countries into their organization:

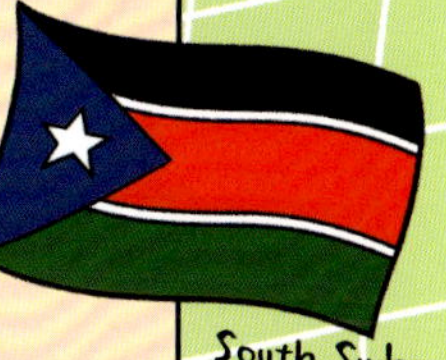

Country	Voted in
East Timor	2005
Montenegro	2007
South Sudan	2012
Kosovo	2016
Gibraltar	2016

OCT 5

MORE TEAMS THAN COUNTRIES

FIFA has more members (211) than there are countries in the United Nations (193). That is because FIFA used to allow dependent territories – a region without full independence from the mother country – to become members. These include territories like Aruba (part of the Netherlands), Puerto Rico (USA), Faroe Islands (Denmark) and Tahiti (France). The four countries that make up the United Kingdom – England, Scotland, Wales and Northern Ireland – also have their own separate teams despite not being fully independent from each other.

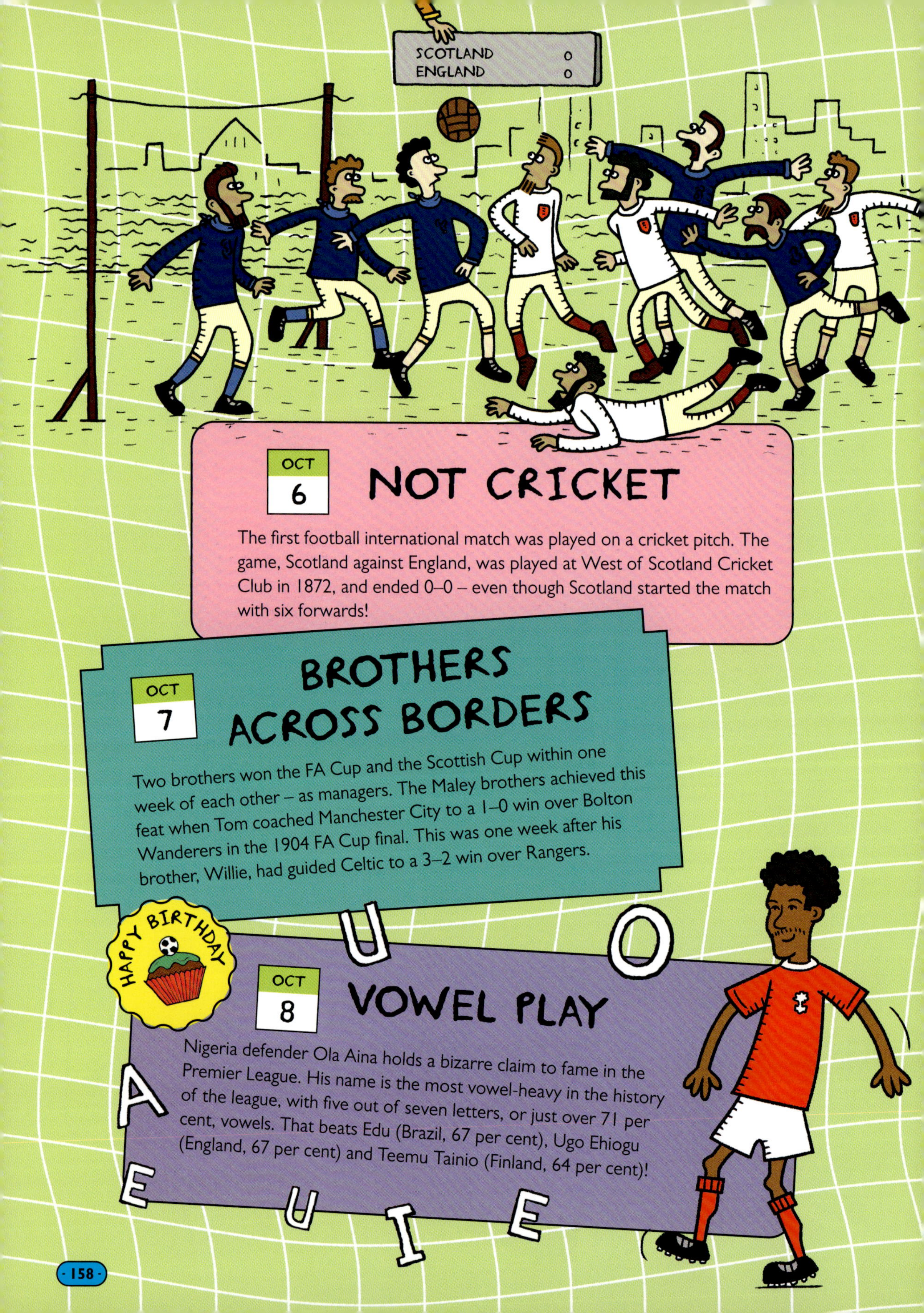

OCT 6

NOT CRICKET

The first football international match was played on a cricket pitch. The game, Scotland against England, was played at West of Scotland Cricket Club in 1872, and ended 0–0 – even though Scotland started the match with six forwards!

OCT 7

BROTHERS ACROSS BORDERS

Two brothers won the FA Cup and the Scottish Cup within one week of each other – as managers. The Maley brothers achieved this feat when Tom coached Manchester City to a 1–0 win over Bolton Wanderers in the 1904 FA Cup final. This was one week after his brother, Willie, had guided Celtic to a 3–2 win over Rangers.

OCT 8

VOWEL PLAY

Nigeria defender Ola Aina holds a bizarre claim to fame in the Premier League. His name is the most vowel-heavy in the history of the league, with five out of seven letters, or just over 71 per cent, vowels. That beats Edu (Brazil, 67 per cent), Ugo Ehiogu (England, 67 per cent) and Teemu Tainio (Finland, 64 per cent)!

SUPER COOPER

Ipswich Town goalkeeper Paul Cooper set a record in 1980 for saving eight of the ten penalties he faced. His tactic was to look like he was about to jump in one direction, encouraging the kicker to kick to the other side. He then switched his dive direction at the last moment to save the penalty. After a few saves, players became much more nervous when they came up against him, which also made it harder for them to score.

GLOVES OFF

In a bid to distract England's penalty-taker in a shoot-out in the Euro 2004 quarter-final, Portugal goalkeeper Ricardo ripped off his gloves and threw them away. His tactic worked: bare-handed, he saved Darius Vassell's penalty and then took, and scored, the next penalty to knock out England.

OCT 11

FAMILY BUSINESS

The only goalkeeper to play for Denmark more often than Kasper Schmeichel (111 games at the time of writing) is his father, Peter (129). Since Denmark played their very first match in 1908, one of the Schmeichels has been in goal in more than a quarter of their matches.

OCT 12

MO-MENTUM

When Mo Salah helped Liverpool beat Glasgow Rangers 7–1 in a 2022 Champions League group match, he scored the quickest hat-trick in Champions League history. His three goals came in just six minutes and twelve seconds, beating the eight-minute record set by Lyon striker Bafétimbi Gomis in 2011.

OCT 13

TOPSY-TURVY TABLE

AIK Stockholm won the Swedish top-division title in 1998, despite scoring the fewest goals of every team in the league. They scored 25 goals in 26 games, but only conceded fifteen goals. At the other end of the table, Manchester City were relegated from England's first division in 1938 despite scoring 80 goals, more than the other 21 teams in the league.

OCT 14

STILL YOUNG

English coach Will Still was the youngest coach in a top-flight league in Europe in 2024. Still was only 29 years old when he was put in charge of French team Reims, who he led to a nineteen-match unbeaten run. But he had not yet started the top coaching qualification, the UEFA Pro Licence, so Reims had to pay a fine of £22,000 for every game he was in charge. Still was so good that Reims thought he was worth it!

OCT 15

OWL HAVE A SLICE

Sheffield Wednesday made a football cake to celebrate their 150th birthday and it smashed the record for the world's largest cake ball in history, weighing in at an incredible 285 kg (the previous record was 54 kg). This is about the weight of 100 bricks – or 650 footballs. The recipe included over 4,000 eggs, and the cake was shared between 15,000 fans who visited the club on the day.

OCT 16

PUNCHY PLAYER

Zambia forward Barbra Banda used to be a professional boxer, winning four of her five fights by a knockout. When she decided to move into football, she became one of the best strikers in the world: she made history in 2020 by becoming the first woman in Olympic history to score hat-tricks in consecutive matches. She still packs a punch!

OCT 17

FROM STANDS TO SCORESHEET

Sarah Crilly scored on her Scotland debut aged 20 – after watching the first half of the game as a supporter from the stands. Crilly played for Hamilton Ladies and had trained with the senior Scotland squad in the week before the 2012 game because they were short of players. At half-time, Crilly was called down from the stands because of an injury crisis. In borrowed kit and wearing boots two sizes too big (plus three pairs of socks), Crilly came on and scored in a 2–2 draw with Norway. "I must have looked ridiculous," she said. "I couldn't believe it when I scored."

OCT 18

UR AMAZING!

Only eight countries have ever won the men's World Cup. In terms of population, Uruguay is by far the smallest of the eight to win it. Here are the winners and their current populations:

Country	Year won World Cup	Population
Uruguay	1930, 1950	3.5 million
Argentina	1978, 1986, 2022	46 million
Spain	2010	49 million
England	1966	56 million
Italy	1934, 1938, 1982, 2006	59 million
West Germany	1954, 1974, 1990	63 million*
France	1998, 2018	68 million
Germany	2014	85 million
Brazil	1958, 1962, 1970, 1994, 2002	216 million

*West Germany and East Germany united to become Germany in 1990.

OCT 19

CHAMP CHOON

The Champions League theme tune is played before every Champions League match. The song is an adaptation by Tony Britten of George Frideric Handel's famous work "Zadok the Priest". UEFA asked Britten to include UEFA's three official languages: English, German and French. Here are the song lyrics!

Die Meister[1]
The champions[2]
Die Besten[3]
Les grandes équipes[4]

[1] "The champions" in German
[2] "The champions" in English
[3] "The best" in German
[4] "The top teams" in French

OCT 20

BOY OH BOY

Newell's Old Boys is famous for being the Argentinian club based in Rosario that Lionel Messi supported, and where he began his career. Between the ages of six and twelve, Messi scored almost 500 goals for their youth team. The club is named after Isaac Newell, an Englishman whose son Claudio founded the club in 1903. Maybe that youth team should have been renamed Messi's Young Boys!

OCT 21

AULD SILVER

The Scottish Cup trophy is the oldest trophy still in use in the history of football. The competition still uses the silver, 61-cm-high trophy that it first gave out in 1873. The FA Cup predates the Scottish Cup, but the English trophy was redesigned in 1911.

OCT 22

CHAMPIONS OF EVERYTHING

The only team to be world champions, continental champions and Olympic champions at the same time is the USA women's team. They held these titles at the same time twice: once between July 2015 and August 2016, and then again between July and September 2000.

OCT 23

HAPPY BIRTHDAY

FOR HE'S A PELÉ GOOD FELLOW

When Pelé was born in 1940, he was given the first name Edson after Thomas Edison, the American inventor of the lightbulb, because his Brazilian village had only just got electricity.

TRIPLE CROWN

Pelé is the first (and at the time of writing, the only) player to win three men's World Cup titles: in 1958, 1962 and 1970. He scored in the 1958 and 1970 finals, but was injured in Brazil's second game in the 1962 tournament and played no further part. As he was part of the squad, he is still allowed to claim the title as a 1962 champion!

BRONZE HERO

More statues have been built in honour of Pelé than any other footballer in the world. There are seventeen statues of the Brazilian, most of them in his homeland. There are also three Pelé statues in India, and one each in China and Ukraine. (Maradona comes next with twelve; Messi and Cruyff have five each.)

OCT 24

COLOUR IN LEEDS

The Leeds squad of 2012–13 contained the most colourful players, by surname, of any English team. The players were Aidy White, Andy Gray, Michael Brown and Paul Green.

OCT 25

THROWING LEGEND

Ireland defender Megan Campbell has a not-so-secret weapon that opponents hate: her long throw. Campbell can hurl the ball an astonishing 38 metres – further than the longest average throw of any male player in Europe's top five leagues. She says her throw is down to hyper-mobile arms that can go back further than the average person.

OCT 26

MAN NEW

Manchester United was originally called Newton Heath and first played in white shirts with a blue trim before changing their name, and the kit to red, in 1902. Newton Heath was the area in Manchester where the club, established for the local railway workers to play against other rail companies, was first based.

OCT 27

GREEN STAR

Norway midfielder Morten Thorsby is football's greenest footballer: he even wears the number two shirt (rare for a player in his position) to remind people about the UN target to keep global warming below 2°C. Thorsby's We Play Green foundation has won awards for its campaigns to protect the environment amid an increase in flooded pitches and rising temperatures.

OCT 28

FISHY TALE

The term *makrellfotball*, meaning mackerel football, is used in Norway to describe a team that plays perfectly in sync with each other. It was originally used to describe the brilliant IK Start team of the 1970s, who played with such co-ordination that they were said to move like a shoal of fish.

OCT 29

SHRIMPLE DEAL

When third division Norwegian side Fløy asked how much it would cost to buy striker Kenneth Kristensen from rivals Vindbjart, they received a fishy response. Vindbjart asked for the player's bodyweight in prawns. Kristensen weighed in at 75 kg, and the deal was done.

GOAL OF THE (20TH) CENTURY

HAPPY BIRTHDAY

Diego Maradona's second goal against England in the 1986 World Cup quarter-final was voted as FIFA's Goal of the Century. He dribbled from inside his own half past five opponents before scoring. When his team-mate Jorge Valdano asked why he didn't pass to him, he replied: "I was going to, but every time I tried, another Englishman appeared, so I went past him."

CHURCH OF MARADONA

Maradona has a religion named after him – the Church of Maradona – and its members worship Maradona as God. It celebrates the two most important days in his life: his birthday and 22 June, the date of his two goals against England in the 1986 World Cup quarter-final. The Church has over 80,000 members and Maradona fans have even got married at the altar. "It's logical," says one of the church's founders, Hernán Amez. "Football is a religion to Argentinians; every religion has its god and the god of football is Diego."

BENFICA CURSE

Portuguese giants Benfica have lost EIGHT finals in a row in European competitions, more than any other club. Some fans believe that this is the result of a curse placed by former coach Béla Guttmann, who guided the team to two European Cup wins in a row, in 1961 and 1962. When his request for a pay rise was refused, he left and said, "Not in a hundred years from now will Benfica ever be European champions." Since then, Benfica has lost five European Cup finals, and three more in other European competitions. Guttmann's curse has come true … so far!

KING ERIKSEN

Denmark midfielder Christian Eriksen came back from the dead after his heart stopped beating during a match against Finland at Euro 2020. Eriksen collapsed on the pitch and was resuscitated by fast-thinking team-mates and doctors. He was later fitted with a defibrillator inside his heart, which keeps it beating regularly. Incredibly, Christian played top-level football again, even starting for Denmark at Euro 2024.

THE GHOST OF SPURS

John White was a talented Scottish winger nicknamed "The Ghost" for the way he floated past defenders. He was part of Tottenham Hotspur's most successful team, which won the League and FA Cup double in 1961. Three years later, while playing golf on his own during a thunderstorm, he took shelter under a tree and was struck by lightning and killed. He was only 27.

RACING CATS

After a 34-year trophy drought, Reinaldo Merlo, the coach of Racing Club, a team in Argentina, demanded that their pitch be dug up to find the bones of a dead cat. Merlo heard the story that, 30 years previously, supporters of local rivals Independiente had buried seven dead cats in their stadium. After thirteen years with no success, six cats were found buried under one goal. But one remained. Merlo insisted the missing seventh cat be found, which it finally was, buried behind the goal at one end of the pitch. One year later, Racing was crowned Argentinian champion again.

OCTOBER QUIZ

1. **Where was the first football international match, between Scotland and England, played in 1872?**
   a) On a cricket pitch in Scotland
   b) On a hockey pitch in England
   c) On a football pitch in Wales
   d) On a polo pitch in Ireland

2. **Place the following countries that have won the World Cup in order according to their population, with the smallest first:**
   a) Brazil
   b) Italy
   c) England
   d) Uruguay
   e) Spain
   f) Germany
   g) Argentina
   h) France

3. **Which player has had the most statues made in their honour?**
   a) Diego Maradona
   b) Lucy Bronze
   c) Pelé
   d) Johan Cruyff

4. **How did Zambia forward Barbra Banda make history at the 2020 Olympic Games?**
   a) She scored hat-tricks in consecutive matches.
   b) She scored a penalty and saved a penalty in the same game.
   c) She scored two Olimpico goals, direct from corner kicks.
   d) She scored the football tournament's first goal and last goal.

5. **How far can Ireland defender Megan Campbell throw a ball?**
   a) 10 metres
   b) 24 metres
   c) 61 metres
   d) 38 metres

6. **Which lyric does NOT appear in the Champions League theme song?**
   a) The champions
   b) The greatest
   c) The best
   d) The top teams

Answers: 1. a, 2. d), g), e), c), b), h), f), a), 3. c, 4. a, 5. d, 6. b

NOVEMBER
15
15

NOVEMBER BIRTHDAYS

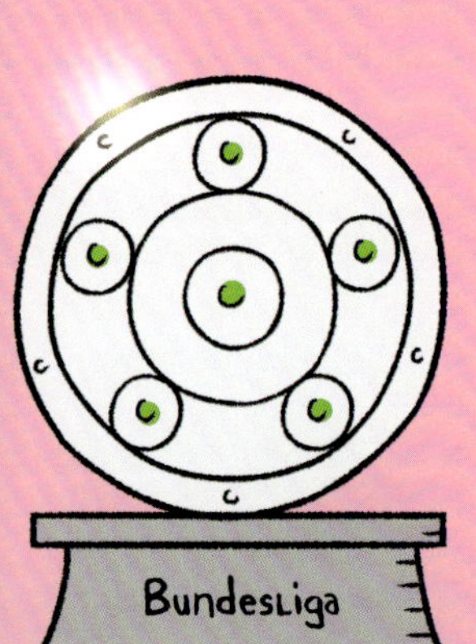

ALPHONSO DAVIES

Canada captain and five-time Bundesliga champion

SANDRA PAÑOS

Spain goalkeeper and two-time Women's Champions League winner with Barcelona

EDUARDO CAMAVINGA

France midfielder, won two Champions Leagues with Real Madrid

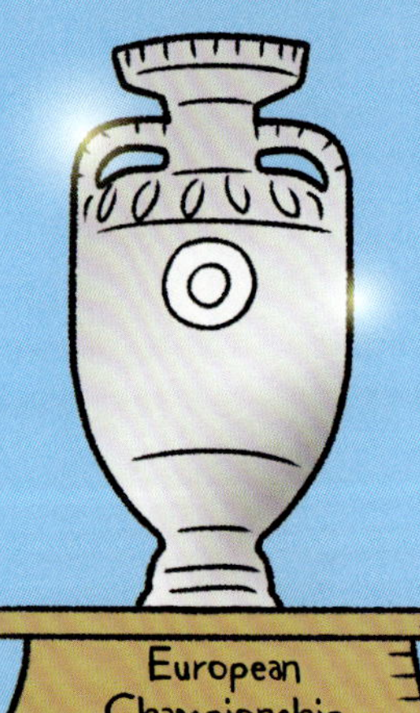

SALMA PARALLUELO

Spanish forward and winner of the Women's U-17, U-20 and World Cup

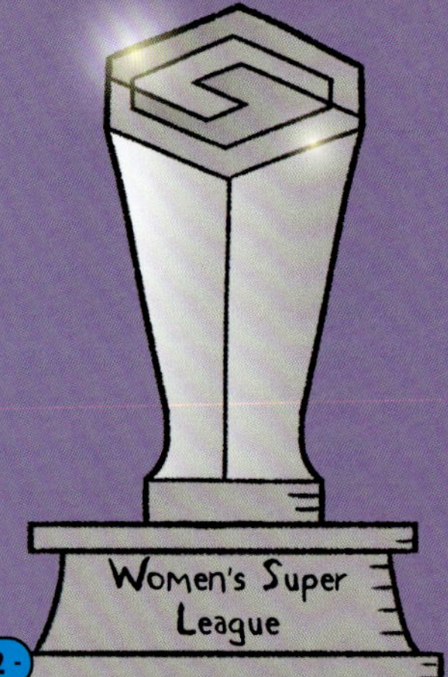

PERNILLE HARDER

Denmark women's all-time leading scorer, won nine league titles in Sweden, Germany and England

LAURENT BLANC

France centre-back, won the 1998 World Cup

RICO LEWIS

England defender and two-time Premier League winner

XABI ALONSO

Spain midfielder, won the Champions League with Liverpool and Real Madrid and coached Bayer Leverkusen to a surprise Bundesliga title

PEDRI

La Liga winner with Barcelona, played for Spain at Euro 2020 aged eighteen

ROBERTO MANCINI

Former Italy forward who coached his country to success at Euro 2020

ALDAIR

Brazil defender, won the 1994 World Cup

NOV 1

WE NEED A BIGGER SCOREBOARD

These are the biggest wins in World Cup matches:

Men's World Cup		
1982	Hungary vs El Salvador	10–1
1954	Hungary vs South Korea	9–0
1974	Yugoslavia vs Zaire	9–0

Women's World Cup		
2019	USA vs Thailand	13–0
2007	Germany vs Argentina	11–0
2015	Germany vs Ivory Coast	10–0

NOV 2

NO SPACE FOR STEFAN

Stefan Schwarz is the first player to have a contract forbidding him from travelling into space. He was keen on space travel and, in 1999, his new club Sunderland were worried something might go wrong if he ventured into space. He is also the only player with initials starting with the same letter who played for a Premier League club and country that also begin with that same letter: Sunderland and Sweden. Sssssssuper!

NOV 3

SILLY SWAN

Swansea mascot, Cyril the Swan, got into trouble after a fight with his Millwall counterpart, Zampa the Lion, in 2001. Cyril and Zampa came to blows after a half-time penalty shoot-out. Cyril ended up punching Zampa's head clean off him and kicked it into the crowd. Cyril had earlier been fined for running onto the pitch while celebrating a goal.

NOV 4

ZIZOU LOSES HEAD

French midfielder Zinedine Zidane was one of the most successful footballers in history – he won the 1998 Ballon d'Or – yet his most famous strike was a violent act during his final match as a player. Playing for France against Italy in the 2006 World Cup final, he headbutted an opponent in the chest and was sent off. It was his last action on the pitch as he retired after the game.

NOV 5

ON YER BIKE

The overhead kick – known as a bicycle kick because the leg motion looks like someone riding a bike upside down – remains one of the most jaw-dropping pieces of skill to excite fans. The first player to use it in a match even has a statue built in his honour! Chile player Ramón Unzaga pulled off the trick in 1914 – and later he scored a bicycle kick against Argentina.

NOV 6

DOUBLE OLIMPICO

An Olimpico is a goal scored directly from a corner and is named after Argentinian winger Cesáreo Onzari, who did just that in a 2–1 win over reigning Olympic champions Uruguay in 1924. The only player to score two Olimpico goals in the Olympic Games is USA winger Megan Rapinoe, in 2012 and 2020.

NOV 7

ROLL LIKE ERLEND

Erlend Fagerli is the greatest freestyle footballer of all time. The Norwegian retired in 2023 after winning ten World Football Freestyle Championships. His most famous move is the Erlend Roll, when he kicks the ball up, flips himself forward and rolls the ball down the back of his legs to the back of his feet, which flick the ball up again. It's even harder than it sounds!

NOV 8

SOMEWHERE OVER THE RAINBOW

The rainbow flick move was popularized by Neymar Jr. It involves cradling the ball against one heel with one foot and then flicking the ball up with the heel, over an opponent's head, and running past them to collect it. Defenders hate this trick: one of Neymar's flicks resulted in an on-pitch brawl as the defenders were so annoyed with him. When he once rainbow-flicked a defender in France, the referee harshly booked him for unsporting behaviour. Unsurprisingly, the inventor of the rainbow flick is also a Brazilian who played for Neymar's first club, Santos. Alexandre de Carvalho Kaneko first pulled off the move in 1968.

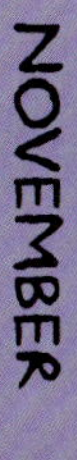

NOV 9 DUN-DEARY ME...

In Nigeria's Yoruba language, the phrase "Dundee United" is an insult meaning "idiot". It originates from the Scottish team's disastrous tour of Nigeria in 1972 – Dundee United lost all their matches and moaned about everything. What a Dundee-saster!

NOV 10 CENTURY BOYS

Iran striker Ali Daei became the first player to score 100 goals in men's international football in 2004. The next two players to hit the 100 mark were Cristiano Ronaldo and Lionel Messi – not bad company for Daei, who briefly played for Bayern Munich, to keep!

NOV 11 BUSY DAY AT THE OFFICE

Striker Mark Hughes once played for his country and his club on the same day. In 1987, he played 90 minutes for Wales in their European Championship qualifying defeat against Czechoslovakia in Prague. Straight after, he was driven to an airport and flown to nearby Germany so he could play in a cup tie for Bayern Munich against Borussia Mönchengladbach. He changed kits on the plane, arrived at half-time and came on as a substitute with his team 1–0 down. Bayern went on to win 3–1 and Hughes was hailed as a hero, even though he was so exhausted that he kept missing the ball and falling over!

NOV 12 SHAQ'S SUPER SIX

Swiss midfielder Xherdan Shaqiri is the first player to score in six successive international tournaments. His first came in the 2014 World Cup. Then he netted goals at the 2018 and 2022 World Cups as well as the Euros in 2016, 2020 and 2024. Shaqiri scores whenever, wherever, once the tournament has begun!

NOV 13 TRES MUNDIALS!

Salma Paralluelo is the first-ever player to win three different age-group World Cups. Her roll-call of honour began in 2018, when she helped Spain win the Under-17 World Cup. In 2022, the forward scored twice in the final as Spain won the Under-20 World Cup; and in the 2023 Women's World Cup, Paralluelo scored Spain's winning goals in the quarter-final and semi-final and started Spain's win over England in the final. Uno, dos, tres!

NOV 14 RAPPER RAFA

Portugal forward Rafael Leão has a second career – as a rap artist called WAY 45. The striker, whose goals helped AC Milan win the Italian league title in 2022, is the son of a singer and nephew of a DJ. His stage-name, WAY 45, refers to the postcode of the neighbourhood he grew up in. "For me it means: 'Don't forget where you came from,'" he says. "Music allows me to express myself because I'm shy."

NOV 15

THE MYSTERY OF A. C. SMITH

Sir Arthur Conan Doyle, the author of the Sherlock Holmes mystery novels, was the first goalkeeper for the team that became known as Portsmouth. He played under a pseudonym (a made-up name) and called himself A. C. Smith. Mystery solved!

NOV 16

MESSY FOR MESSI

Lionel Messi was sent off less than a minute after his debut for Argentina in 2005 when he was eighteen. After coming on as a substitute, he was dismissed for elbowing Hungary defender Vilmos Vanczák, who now sees his brief meeting with the young star as his claim to fame. "I like it that, at one point in history, we came together. It's a big thing for me!" Vanczák says.

NOV 17

BETTER LETTERS

Rochdale
O'Donnell
Mullarkey
Ebanks-Landell
Taylor
Odoh
Keohane
Brierley
Lloyd-McGoldrick
Dodgson
Henderson
Bughail-Mellor

The team with the longest combined surnames in English football was Rochdale's 103 characters when they played Crawley Town in March 2023 (left). The fewest of 51 characters, was first achieved by Stoke City with the team on the right in 1951 (and later equalled twice by Stoke, and once by Northampton and Stevenage).

Stoke City
Fox
Dixon
Carr
Parkin
Bould
Berry
Ford
Daly
Morgan
Shaw
Heath

NOV 18

A LONG WAIT

Some national teams have waited a long time since lifting their most recent trophy – whether it's a World Cup or continental championship like the Euros. Here are the teams that have had the longest wait.

Team	Last success	Trophy
Russia	1960	European Championship
South Korea	1960	Asian Cup
Ethiopia	1962	Africa Cup of Nations
Bolivia	1963	Copa América
Israel	1964	Asian Cup
England	1966	World Cup
Guatemala	1967	CONCACAF Championship

My dad wasn't even born when we last won a trophy

Neither was my gran!

SPORTS TIMES
USA WIN

WORLD CUP TRIUMPH

USA BUGLE
EPIC PENAL WIN

SPORTS WEEK
BRILLIANT BRANDI

INSPIRED

FOOT FEAT

Brandi Chastain scored USA's winning penalty in the 1999 World Cup final – with her weaker foot! The defender needed to score to win the trophy. She normally took penalties with her right foot but her coach, Tony DiCicco, advised her to kick the penalty with her left foot, to provide more accuracy. Chastain kicked with her left foot … and scored! The image of her celebration, with her shirt off and pumping her fists, inspired a generation of female players.

NOV 20

LEAGUE STRANGLEHOLD

The longest unbroken sequence of two teams continuing to win the league in Europe is still going on in Scotland. Glasgow giants Rangers and Celtic have won every league title since 1985, a run that's eight years longer than in any other European league. Here are the other countries with two dominant teams:

League	Teams	Years won	Run started	Previous winner
Scotland	Celtic, Rangers	40*	1985	Aberdeen
Ukraine	Shakhtar D, Dynamo K	31	1993	Tavriya Simferopol
Scotland	Celtic, Rangers	27	1904	Third Lanark
Serbia	Crvena Zvezda**, Partizan	26	1998	Obilić
Hungary	Ferencváros, MTK Budapest	24	1903	Budapesti Torna Club

*This run continues at the time of writing.

**Formerly known as Red Star.

NOV 21

BIG FISH, LITTLE FISH

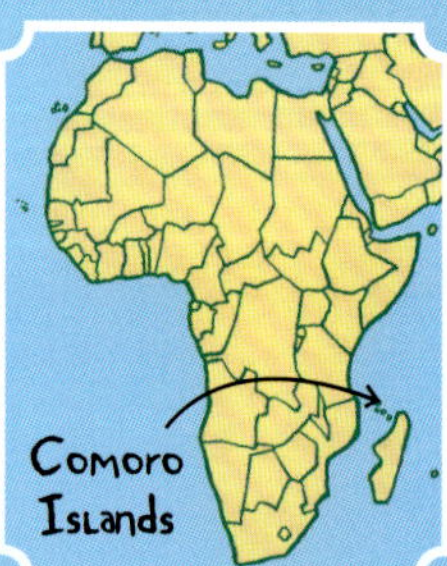

The football team of the tiny island nation of Comoros are nicknamed the Coelacanths, a critically-endangered species of fish. In 2021, the team qualified for the Africa Cup of Nations for the first time. In the group stage, they caused a huge shock by beating four-time winners Ghana, which has 40 times the population. They qualified for the knockout round and faced another of the continent's big teams, Cameroon. However, just before the match the Comoros squad was hit by an illness which ruled out twelve players – including all three of their goalkeepers – which meant defender Chaker Alhadhur had to play the full match in goal! They lost to Cameroon, the eventual champions, 2–1, a tiny margin considering their disadvantages.

NOV 22

CURVE BALL

Alex loves maths, so for his birthday here is his favourite football geometry fact. The original shape of the goal area looked like a B, because the goal kick had to be taken no further than six yards from either goal-post. The two curved parts are made up of points six yards from each post. These markings lasted from 1891 to 1902, when the current format of an eighteen-yard penalty area, penalty spot twelve yards from goal and a goal area of six yards out was introduced.

NOV 23

ON TARGET

New Zealand striker Hannah Wilkinson is also a mural artist who created an amazing image to celebrate her country hosting World Cups in cricket, rugby and football at the Eden Park national stadium. In the first game at the 2023 Women's World Cup, she scored New Zealand's winning goal against Norway – at Eden Park!

NOV 24

ATHLETIC WILL-BAO!

Brothers Iñaki and Nico Williams were both part of the Athletic Bilbao team that won the 2024 Spanish Cup final – while in international football, they play for different countries. Iñaki represents Ghana, where his parents come from, and Nico plays for Spain, where he was born. At Euro 2024, Nico set another record: the youngest player, since records began in 1980, to score a goal, assist with a goal and successfully complete all of his passes in one game. Nico scored Spain's opening goal in their final win over England.

NOV 25

VICTORY LAPS

Lapland, playing under its preferred name of Sápmi, won the first-ever World Cup for regions and states that are unrecognized by FIFA. Held in 2006, Sápmi represented the Sámi people who live in northern areas of Norway, Sweden, Finland and Russia. They beat Monaco 21–1 in the final, and two of their goalscorers went on to represent Norway.

NOV 26

SAUSAGE MINUTE

Finland top-division side SJK Seinäjoki agreed to give away free sausages to the crowd if they scored in the 77th minute as part of a sponsorship tie-in with a company that sells sausages which contain 77 per cent meat. The crowd sang, "Sausages! Sausages!" when the time came, and in May 2024, against Inter Turku, striker Rasmus Karjalainen scored during the Sausage Minute!

NOV 27

HANDY IN THE SANDY

Since the Beach Soccer World Cup began in 2005, Brazil has won more tournaments than anyone else. It may be helped by having over 2,000 beaches in the country, including the longest uninterrupted sandy beach in the world: Praia do Cassino, which runs for over 200 km. Now that's a long pitch!

NOV 28

JUST AMAZING

France striker Just Fontaine holds the record for most goals scored in a single World Cup, when he scored thirteen goals in six games in 1958. His achievement is all the more remarkable because he had only scored once for France in the previous four years – and in 1958, he was not wearing his own boots, but had to borrow a pair from his team-mate!

NOV 29

HIGH FIVE!

Brazilian striker Marta is the first player to score at five different World Cups and has scored more World Cup goals than any other player. Despite that, she has never won a World Cup – the closest she came was in 2007, when Brazil faced Germany in the final. With Germany leading 1–0, Brazil won a penalty. Marta stepped up … but her effort was saved. Germany won the game 2–0 and Brazil, with Marta in the team, never reached the final again.

NOV 30

GOODIE GARY

One of England's greatest-ever players, Gary Lineker, played 654 games and never received a yellow or red card. The forward scored 48 goals for England and won the Golden Boot in the 1986 World Cup. He explained his dad removed him from a match after he questioned the referee when he was fourteen – and he's been on his best behaviour ever since!

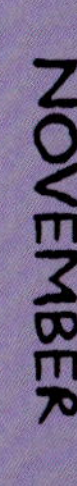

NOVEMBER QUIZ

1. **France midfielder Zinedine Zidane retired after playing in the 2006 World Cup final. What was his final act on a football pitch?**
   a) Scoring a penalty in the successful shoot-out
   b) Lifting the World Cup trophy
   c) Limping off injured in extra-time
   d) Being sent off after headbutting an opponent

2. **Who is Erlend Fagerli?**
   a) The inventor of the bicycle-kick
   b) The greatest freestyle footballer of all time
   c) The designer of the centre-circle
   d) The founder of the Church of Diego Maradona

3. **What World Cup record does Brazil striker Marta hold?**
   a) She has won more World Cups than any other player.
   b) She has scored more World Cup goals than any other player.
   c) She has played in more World Cup games than any other player.
   d) She has missed more World Cup penalties than any other player.

4. **Lionel Messi made his Argentina debut against Hungary in 2005. What happened in the game?**
   a) Messi was sent off.
   b) Messi scored a hat-trick.
   c) Messi set up three goals.
   d) Messi was subbed off after fifteen minutes.

5. **What is Lapland's footballing claim to fame?**
   a) They won the first World Cup for regions that are not recognized by FIFA.
   b) They have a team called Santa Claus FC.
   c) Erling Haaland was born there.
   d) Coaches sit on reindeer during matches.

6. **Which trophy-winning national team has had the longest wait to win another trophy?**
   a) Bolivia
   b) England
   c) Russia
   d) South Korea

Answers: 1. d, 2. b, 3. b, 4. a, 5. a, 6. c

DECEMBER

DECEMBER BIRTHDAYS
Centre-forward
Left-wing
Right-wing
Left-midfield
Centre-midfield
Right-midfield
Left-back
Centre-back
Centre-back
Right-back
Fir he's a holly good fellow...
Did you know the Christmas tree formation was first used in English football by Crystal Palace in 1970?
Goal-keeper

DEC 20
KYLIAN MBAPPÉ
First teenager to win the World Cup since Pelé, scored hat-trick in the 2022 World Cup final
DEC 29
CHRISTEN PRESS
Two-time Women's World Cup winner in 2015 and 2019 with USA
DEC 6
RACHEL DALY
Star who plays in many positions, helped England win Euro 2022
DEC 24
ALEXIS MAC ALLISTER
Argentina midfielder who set up a goal in the 2022 World Cup final
DEC 17
MARTIN ØDEGAARD
Mercurial midfielder, made first appearance for Norway aged fifteen
DEC 20
JARROD BOWEN
England player, scored West Ham's winning goal in the 2023 Europa Conference League final
DEC 17
WESLEY FOFANA
France defender who helped Leicester win the 2021 FA Cup
DEC 19
FIKAYO TOMORI
England defender who won the 2022 Serie A with AC Milan
DEC 21
BEN CHILWELL
England defender who helped Chelsea win the 2021 Champions League
DEC 30
GORDON BANKS
England goalkeeper who won the 1966 World Cup
DEC 8
REECE JAMES
Chelsea captain and runner-up at Euro 2020 with England

DEC 1

TWINNED

Identical twins Benjamin and Marco Zürcher always work together during matches: as referees' assistants on either side of the pitch. The duo run the lines in the Swiss league, and in 2024 were promoted to officiate in the Champions League. Double trouble!

DEC 2

THIS ONE'S A KEEPER

USA's Mia Hamm is the only outfield player to have ever played in goal in a World Cup match. Her time between the posts came in 1995 when USA goalkeeper, Briana Scurry, was sent off late on against Denmark. USA was leading 2–0 and Hamm saw out the edgy final stages without conceding a goal. She described her period in goal as "the longest eleven minutes of my life".

DEC 3

HOWDY STRANGER!

Owen Hargreaves is the only player to play for England without ever having lived in the country before his first appearance. Hargreaves had a Welsh mother and English father, but was born in Canada. He moved to Germany aged sixteen to play for Bayern Munich, winning the Champions League with them in 2001. A few months later he made his England debut, the first of 42 appearances for his country.

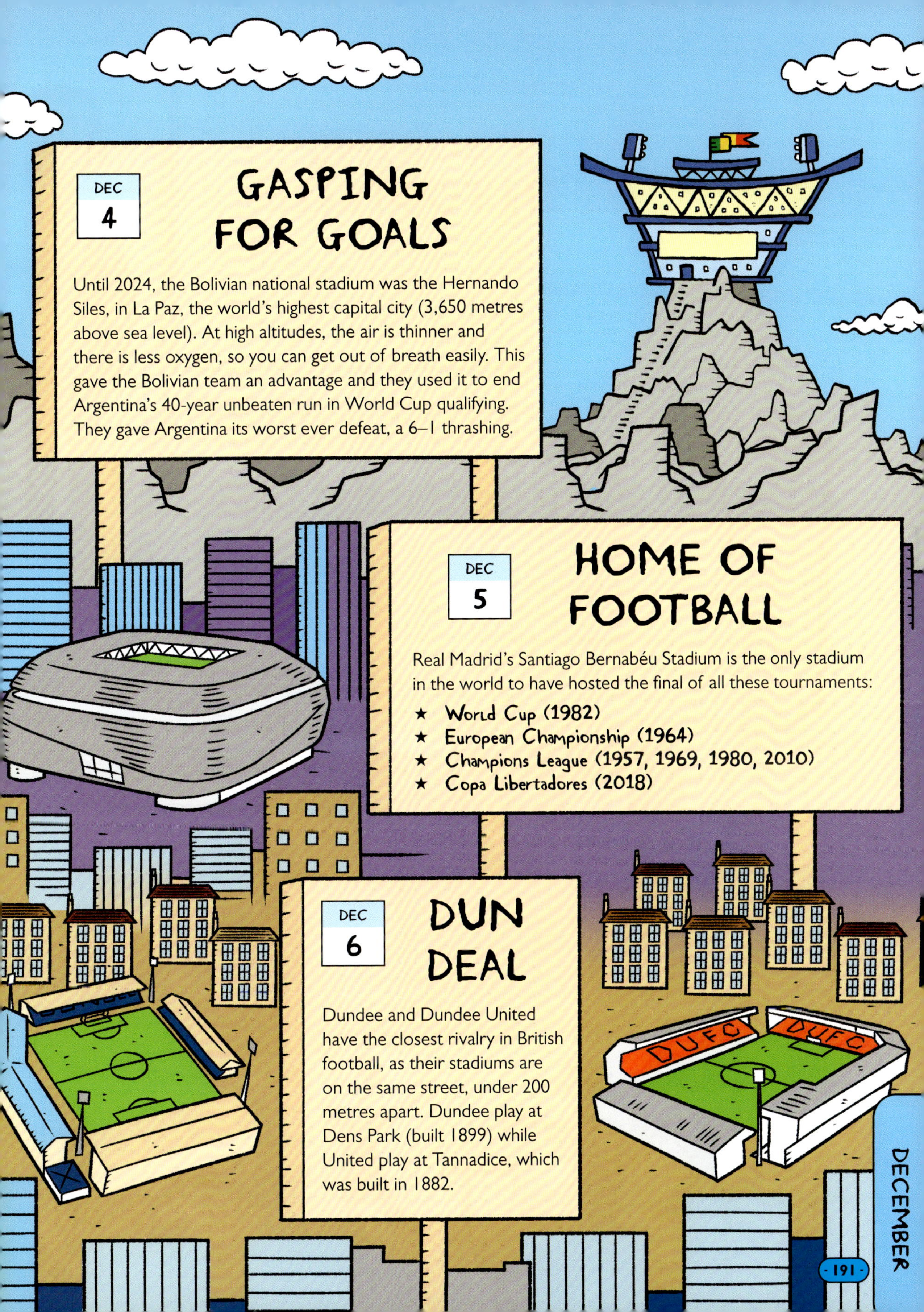

GASPING FOR GOALS

DEC 4

Until 2024, the Bolivian national stadium was the Hernando Siles, in La Paz, the world's highest capital city (3,650 metres above sea level). At high altitudes, the air is thinner and there is less oxygen, so you can get out of breath easily. This gave the Bolivian team an advantage and they used it to end Argentina's 40-year unbeaten run in World Cup qualifying. They gave Argentina its worst ever defeat, a 6–1 thrashing.

HOME OF FOOTBALL

DEC 5

Real Madrid's Santiago Bernabéu Stadium is the only stadium in the world to have hosted the final of all these tournaments:

- ★ World Cup (1982)
- ★ European Championship (1964)
- ★ Champions League (1957, 1969, 1980, 2010)
- ★ Copa Libertadores (2018)

DUN DEAL

DEC 6

Dundee and Dundee United have the closest rivalry in British football, as their stadiums are on the same street, under 200 metres apart. Dundee play at Dens Park (built 1899) while United play at Tannadice, which was built in 1882.

DEC 7

MOST BORING JOB IN FOOTBALL

Gustavo Matosas resigned as Costa Rica national team coach in 2019 because he was bored. He said he missed seeing his players every day, as he only worked with them for nine international matches in the year he had the job.

DEC 8

DEAN AT THE DOUBLE

England goalkeeper Dean Henderson was 22 years old when he broke two world records – on the same day! The first was for the fastest time to dress as a goalkeeper, putting on his boots, shin-pads, socks, shorts, shirt and gloves in under 49.5 seconds. The second was for the most headed passes in one minute in a team of two, which he completed with England Under-21 team-mate Jake Clarke-Salter. Their total of 91 headers in just 60 seconds is a-head of everyone!

DEC 9

SIMPLESMENTE THE BEST

Spain made history while winning Euro 2024 as the first team to win all seven games they played in the tournament, without needing extra-time or penalties. They also beat four previous World Cup winners (France, Germany, Italy, England) and, in the final, started with ten outfield players from ten different clubs – another first. *Simplesmente* (simply) the best!

DEC 10

NATIONAL TREASURE

Ildefons Lima holds the record for the longest international football career. He made his debut for the Andorra national team in 1997, in only their second-ever game. It was a 4–1 defeat in Estonia and he scored the country's first-ever goal. The centre-back retired in 2023, after 26 years and 137 games – winning six of them!

DEC 11

BAM-BOOTS

Nigeria defender William Troost-Ekong was the first player at a major international tournament to wear football boots made from sustainable materials. The boots, called Sokito Scudetta, which he wore at the 2023 Africa Cup of Nations, had a vegan suede lining and tongue made from corn waste, a sole partly made from castor beans and an insole made from sugarcane and bamboo.

DEC 12

FISHING FOR BALLS

Fred Davis spent 40 years as football's most unique ball boy. Between 1947 and 1987, he worked for Shrewsbury Town, retrieving balls from the nearby River Severn. Davis sat on the river in a wooden tub, known as a coracle, during matches. When a ball was struck over the stands and into the river, he'd spend ten minutes collecting it. He was paid for every ball he retrieved. The club thought it was cheaper to use Fred than to build a fence!

DEC 13

PENALTY PETE

One of Chelsea's most popular players will never be forgotten at their Stamford Bridge stadium – because his ashes are buried under the penalty spot. Peter Osgood was a centre-forward whose goals helped Chelsea win their first-ever FA Cup in 1970.

DEC 14

LOCAL KNOWLEDGE

Many English teams have nicknames based on traditional industries where the clubs are based.

Team	Industry	Nickname
Crewe Alexandra	Railways	Railwaymen
Grimsby	Fishing	Mariners
Luton	Hat-making	Hatters
Macclesfield	Silk	Silkmen
Northampton	Shoemaking	Cobblers

Team	Industry	Nickname
Scunthorpe	Iron	Iron
Sheffield United	Steel	Blades
Stoke City	Pottery	Potters
Walsall	Horse saddle-making	Saddlers
Yeovil	Gloves	Glovers

ON THIS DAY

DEC 15

TED'S TRIUMPH

Arsenal striker Ted Drake scored seven goals on this day in 1935. The Gunners, then reigning league champions, beat Aston Villa 7–1 in a first-division match. The seven-goal haul remains the most goals scored by one player in a top-division game in England.

DEC 16 MOUNTAIN MEN WIN AT LAST

In 2024, football's lowest ranked team, San Marino, won their first competitive match after 34 years and 176 games… And then two months and five games later, they won again! San Marino were at the bottom of the FIFA ranking when they beat Liechtenstein 1–0 in September 2024. The country, a mountainous micro-state in northern Italy with an area smaller than Brighton and a population of 34,000 people, beat Liechtenstein again, 3–1 away from home, later in the same year. This was the first time they had ever scored three goals in one game!

DEC 17 KING LIONEL

When Lionel Messi captained Argentina to success in the 2022 World Cup final, he achieved a succession of firsts, as the first player to:

- Win the Golden Ball (for the tournament's best player) at two different World Cups
- Score in the group stage, round of 16, quarter-final, semi-final and final in the same tournament
- Make 26 appearances in World Cup matches, becoming the all-time record-holder for most games

DEC 18 PERP! PERP!

Swedish defender Adam Lindin Ljungkvist was sent off after being shown a second yellow card for farting on the pitch. The referee claimed it was "a deliberate provocation" and unsportsmanlike behaviour. Ljungkvist denied it was intentional and blamed the fart on a bad tummy.

DEC 19

STAR STUDENT

Germany midfielder Lena Oberdorf was seventeen when she was picked to play in the 2019 Women's World Cup, so she had to take school exams in the middle of the tournament. She became Germany's youngest-ever player at a World Cup – and passed her English and sports exams at the same time. Good work, Lena!

DEC 20

BORN LEADERS

Many players, helped by their fame during their careers, have used their platforms to become politicians once their careers are finished. Here are some examples:

Player	Country	Playing highlight	Politics highlight
Ahmed Ben Bella	Algeria	Scored on Marseille debut	President
George Weah	Liberia	1995 Ballon d'Or winner	President
Kaj Leo Johansen	Faroe Islands	Three Faroes league titles	Prime Minister
Kakha Kaladze	Georgia	Two Champions League titles	Deputy PM
Mikheil Kavelashvili	Georgia	Titles in Georgia, Russia, Switzerland	President

DEC 21

TA-TWO IN ONE!

Finland winger Topi Keskinen has one of the strangest football tattoos: an image of England legend Wayne Rooney fishing. He said he had it done because fishing is his favourite hobby and Rooney is his favourite player.

DEC 22

DANISH DYNAMITE

Denmark won Euro 1992 – even though they did not qualify for the tournament! They were last-minute replacements for Yugoslavia, who were disqualified because of the civil war there. The Danes provided one of the biggest shocks in international football. The team, nicknamed "Danish Dynamite", beat France and the Netherlands on penalties before defeating Germany 2–0 in the final.

DEC 23

THIS ONE'S A BANGER!

English composer Sir Edward Elgar wrote one of the world's first football songs in 1898 after watching his favourite team Wolverhampton Wanderers beat Stoke City. Elgar composed a short piano piece called "He Banged the Leather for Goal", which is how a newspaper described how Wolves striker Billy Malpass took a shot. The piece was performed for the first time in 2010 for charity – over 100 years after it was written!

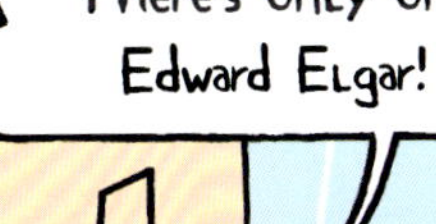

THE CHRISTMAS DAY TRUCE

On Christmas Eve in 1914, German and British soldiers fighting against each other in the First World War agreed to put down their weapons. The next day, they played football together in a remarkable act of togetherness. The kickabout was played in no-man's-land, a space in between the ditches where the soldiers were based. It is not known how many people took part, but the Christmas Day truce showed the power of football to bring people together even in the darkest of times.

DEC
25

DICK, KERR

Dick, Kerr Ladies played their first match on Christmas Day, 1917. About 10,000 fans turned up to watch the female workers from the Dick, Kerr factory play in a match that raised money for the local hospital. At one point, 50,000 fans turned up to watch them play. The team became extremely popular – so much so that, in 1921, the Football Association, worried that the women's game would take money from the men's, banned clubs from allowing women's teams to use their stadiums. The result was effectively a ban on women's football that stayed in place for 50 years.

DEC 26

SNOW JOKE

Bishop Auckland goalkeeper Harry Sharratt was booked during a Boxing Day fixture for building a snowman on the goal-line. Not a cool way to stop the opposition!

DEC 27

BIG SPENDERS

Scottish club Falkirk broke the world transfer record in 1922 when they signed striker "Super" Sydney Puddefoot from West Ham for £5,000. Puddefoot was homesick to start with, so the club signed his brother Len. That didn't help much (Len only played two games). Super Syd stayed for three seasons and scored plenty of goals, but Falkirk did not win a trophy.

DEC 28

SCILLY SEASON

The smallest league in the world is the Isles of Scilly league, off Cornwall, which has two teams in it. The league, based on the island of Saint Mary's, was established in the 1920s and the two teams, Garrison Gunners and Woolpack Wanderers, face each other around 20 times during the season. They also play in two Cup competitions against each other! Often the teams include policemen or firefighters who can be called away mid-match for an emergency. Once a farmer, called Chuffer, had to leave as his cows had escaped their field!

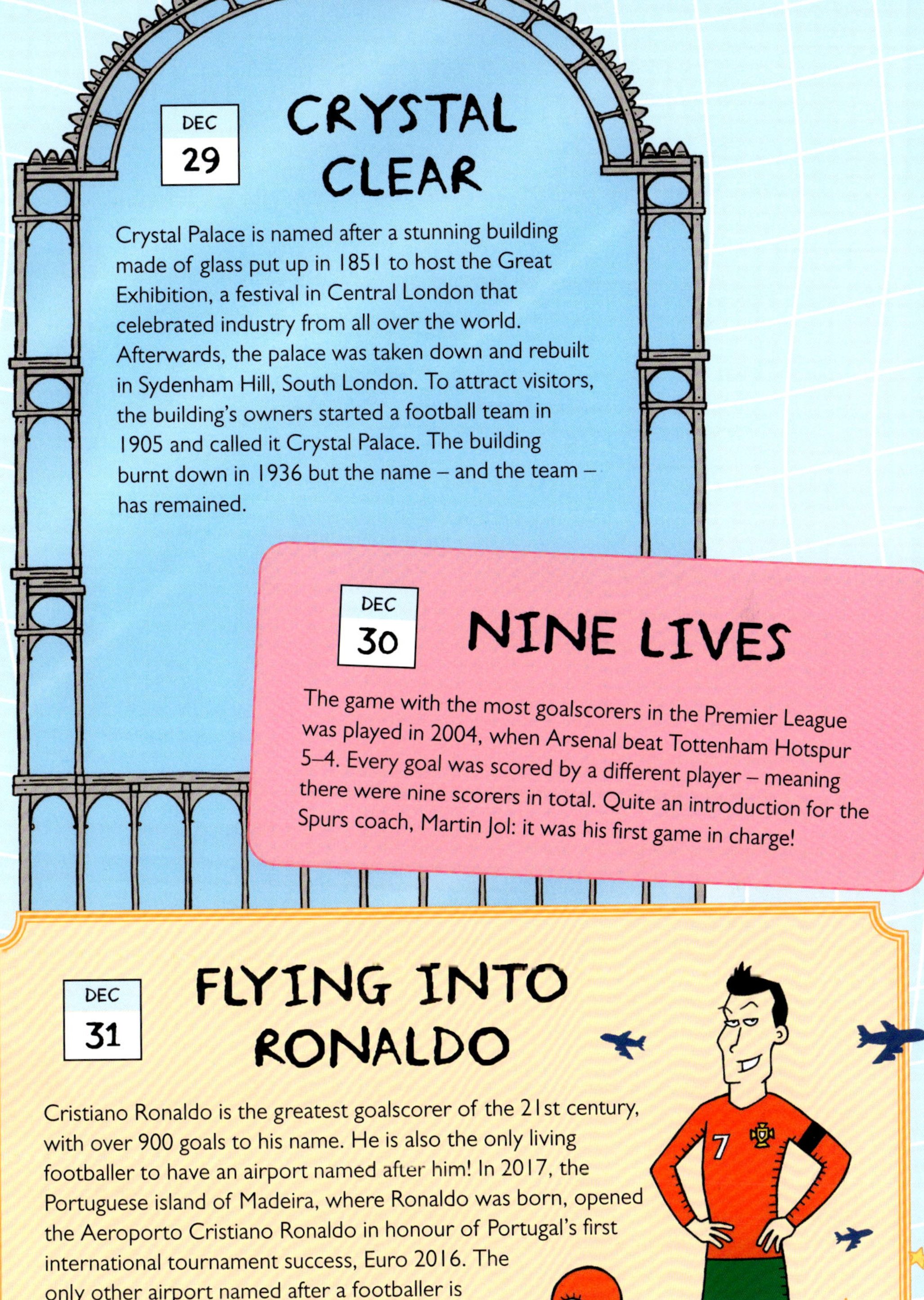

DEC 29

CRYSTAL CLEAR

Crystal Palace is named after a stunning building made of glass put up in 1851 to host the Great Exhibition, a festival in Central London that celebrated industry from all over the world. Afterwards, the palace was taken down and rebuilt in Sydenham Hill, South London. To attract visitors, the building's owners started a football team in 1905 and called it Crystal Palace. The building burnt down in 1936 but the name – and the team – has remained.

DEC 30

NINE LIVES

The game with the most goalscorers in the Premier League was played in 2004, when Arsenal beat Tottenham Hotspur 5–4. Every goal was scored by a different player – meaning there were nine scorers in total. Quite an introduction for the Spurs coach, Martin Jol: it was his first game in charge!

DEC 31

FLYING INTO RONALDO

Cristiano Ronaldo is the greatest goalscorer of the 21st century, with over 900 goals to his name. He is also the only living footballer to have an airport named after him! In 2017, the Portuguese island of Madeira, where Ronaldo was born, opened the Aeroporto Cristiano Ronaldo in honour of Portugal's first international tournament success, Euro 2016. The only other airport named after a footballer is Northern Ireland's George Best Belfast City Airport, which opened in 2006. Like Ronaldo, Best, who died in 2005, also played for Manchester United – and both wore the number seven shirt!

DECEMBER QUIZ

1. What World Cup record does USA midfielder Mia Hamm hold?

a) The only player to win four World Cup finals
b) The only player to play in a World Cup match aged fifteen
c) The only player to score in every World Cup game she played
d) The only outfield player to have played in goal in a World Cup match

2. Which two British clubs have their stadiums on the same street, only 200 metres apart?

a) Nottingham Forest and Notts County
b) Everton and Liverpool
c) Fulham and Chelsea
d) Dundee and Dundee United

3. Why was Swedish defender Adam Lindin Ljungkvist sent off in 2016?

a) Burping at the referee
b) Farting on the pitch
c) Weeing in his shorts
d) Being sick on his boots

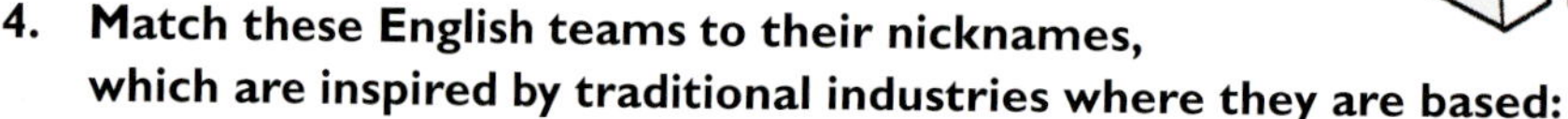

4. Match these English teams to their nicknames, which are inspired by traditional industries where they are based:

a) Stoke City	1. Saddlers
b) Sheffield United	2. Potters
c) Luton	3. Cobblers
d) Walsall	4. Hatters
e) Northampton	5. Blades

5. What is former England midfielder Owen Hargreaves's international claim to fame?

a) The first player to captain England
b) The only player to represent England without having lived there before his debut
c) The first player to score for England in a penalty shoot-out
d) The only player called Owen to ever play for England

6. Finland winger Topi Keskinen combined his favourite player and his favourite hobby to create a tattoo on his arm. What was it?

a) Wayne Rooney fishing
b) Cristiano Ronaldo baking
c) David Beckham painting
d) Jari Litmanen playing the guitar

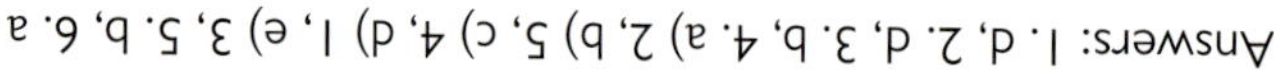

Answers: 1. d, 2. d, 3. b, 4. a) 2, b) 5, c) 4, d) 1, e) 3, 5. b, 6. a

END OF YEAR PUZZLE SUPER CHALLENGE

MANAGER PARLAYS (also known as PLAYER ANAGRAMS)

Can you identify these players from the anagrams of their names?
(As a clue, all of these players appeared in a Birthday Spread at the start of the month in this book)

1. MOLE PARCEL
2. GATEWAY SIGNORA
3. HANKY REAR
4. DIAGONAL GUNKY
5. TEXAS COLT

MATCH OF THE DAY

Here are three match-ups for you:

1. **Match the European gods with the cities whose football teams have the god in their names.**

2. **Match the familiar team names to the countries with title-winning teams who have the same name.**

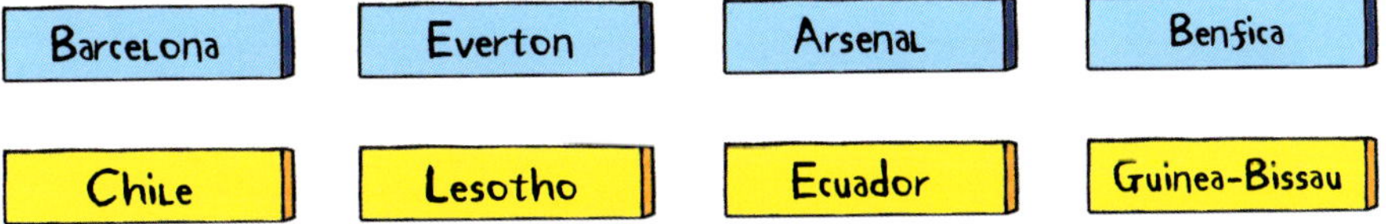

3. **Match the English clubs to the birds they are nicknamed after.**

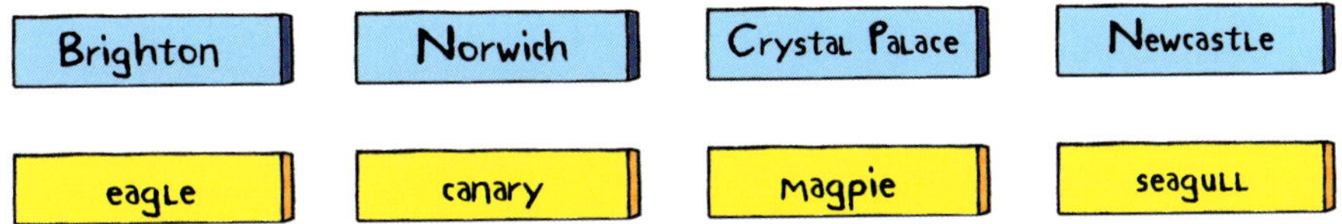

TRUE OR FALSE?

1. Cristiano Ronaldo and David Beckham have airports named after them.
2. England goalkeeper Dean Henderson once broke two world records on the same day.
3. Brazilian club Vasco da Gama is named after the Portuguese explorer.
4. England forward Cole Palmer also qualifies to play for Caribbean island Antigua.
5. South Korea has a football league for players who are over 80.
6. Pop star Sir Elton John is life-president of Watford as he used to own the club.
7. West Bromwich Albion's ground is the highest in England.
8. Teams playing in blue win more games than would be expected.
9. Croatia and Panama are the only international teams to wear kits with checks.
10. Sadio Mané once scored a Premier League hat-trick in under three minutes.

FOOTBALL CONNECTIONS

1. What common thread links each of these four groups of football teams?

a)	Uruguay	France	Italy	Argentina
b)	Preston	Notts County	Accrington	Bolton
c)	AC Milan	Inter Milan	Roma	Napoli
d)	Stoke	Luton	Walsall	Grimsby

2. What common thread links each of these four groups of footballers?

a)	Just Fontaine	Harry Kane	Homare Sawa	Ronaldo
b)	Aldair	Pelé	Garrincha	Ronaldinho
c)	Alf Common	Gareth Bale	Neymar Jr	Jean-Pierre Papin
d)	Nahuel Guzman	Mary Earps	Sir Arthur Conan Doyle	Emi Martínez

ANSWERS

Manager Parlays:

1. MOLE PARCEL = COLE PALMER
2. GATEWAY SIGNORA = GEORGIA STANWAY
3. HANKY REAR = HARRY KANE
4. DIAGONAL GUNKY = ILKAY GUNDOGAN
5. TEXAS COLT = ALEX SCOTT

Match of the Day:

1. Ajax and Amsterdam. Apollo and Limassol. Ares and Thessaloniki. Veles and Moscow.
2. Barcelona and Ecuador. Everton and Chile. Arsenal and Lesotho. Benfica and Guinea-Bissau.
3. Brighton and seagull. Norwich and canary. Crystal Palace and eagle. Newcastle and magpie.

True or False:

1. False (it's George Best, not Beckham). 2. True. 3. True. 4. False (St Kitts & Nevis, not Antigua). 5. False (the league is in Japan). 6. True. 7. True. 8. False (it's true for teams playing in red). 9. False (only Croatia). 10. True.

Football Connections: 1. a) They are all World Cup winners. b) They were in the first football league in 1888. c) They are all Italian teams with a retired shirt number. d) They all have local industry-related nicknames.

2. a) They have all won the World Cup Golden Boot for top scorer. b) They have all won the World Cup with Brazil. c) They have all broken transfer world records. d) They are all goalkeepers.

-ACKNOWLEDGEMENTS-

Time for one more fact: we love Spike Gerrell! Thank you Spike; your fantastic illustrations continue to give life to our words and joy to our life.

Thanks to the brilliant team at Walker Books: Daisy Jellicoe, Denise Johnstone-Burt, Louise Jackson, Rachel Cooke, Faith Leung, Maryam Rimi, Jack Noel and Rebecca Oram. Shout-out to Keiron Ward for your tremendous input. Thanks also to our agent Claire Conrad and her team at Janklow & Nesbit.

In a world where recognizing that facts are more important than ever, we are grateful to our friends and colleagues who helped us source or verify these facts. These include: Martyn Amos, Michael Bar-Eli, Hakan Baş, Tom Burrows, Michael Caley, Felipe Cardenas, Marcus Christenson, Rob Eastaway, Bill Edgar, Nick Harris, Pablo Maurer, James Montague, Ignacio Palacios-Huerta. Alex would like to thank Nat, Zachary and Barnaby. Ben would like to thank Annie, Clemmy and Bibi for their joke-checking and support.

-INDEX-

FOOTBALL SCHOOL
Season 1
WHERE FOOTBALL RULES THE WORLD
ALEX BELLOS BEN LYTTLETON

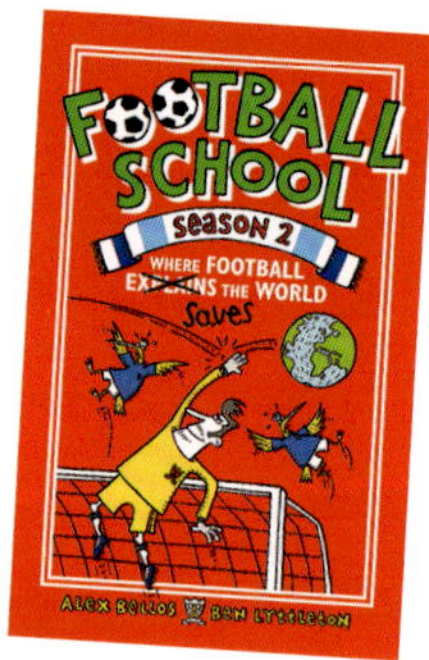
FOOTBALL SCHOOL
Season 2
WHERE FOOTBALL SAVES THE WORLD
ALEX BELLOS BEN LYTTLETON

FOOTBALL SCHOOL
Season 3
WHERE FOOTBALL TACKLES THE WORLD
ALEX BELLOS BEN LYTTLETON

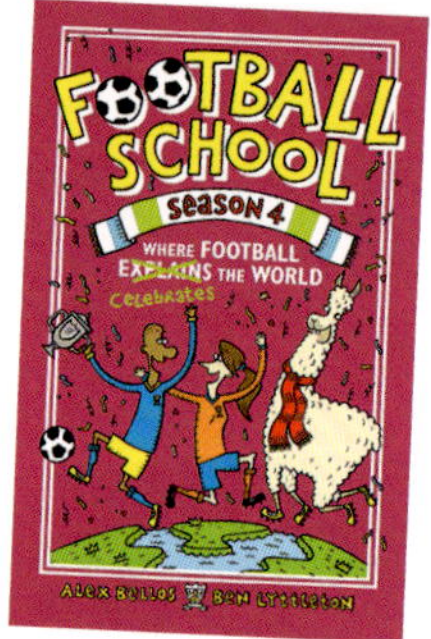
FOOTBALL SCHOOL
Season 4
WHERE FOOTBALL CELEBRATES THE WORLD
ALEX BELLOS BEN LYTTLETON

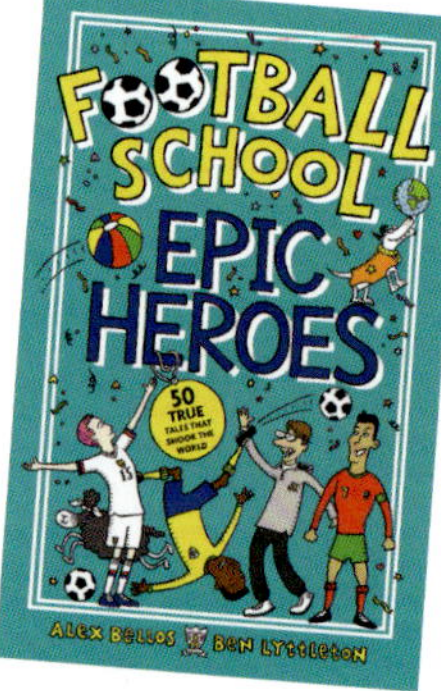
FOOTBALL SCHOOL
EPIC HEROES
50 TRUE TALES THAT SHOOK THE WORLD
ALEX BELLOS BEN LYTTLETON

FOOTBALL SCHOOL
STAR PLAYERS
50 INSPIRING STORIES OF TRUE FOOTBALL HEROES
ALEX BELLOS BEN LYTTLETON

OVER 300 FAN-TASTIC QUESTIONS
FOOTBALL SCHOOL
THE AMAZING QUIZ BOOK
TEST YOUR WORLD CUP KNOWLEDGE!
ALEX BELLOS BEN LYTTLETON

COLLECT THE FOOTBALL SCHOOL SERIES

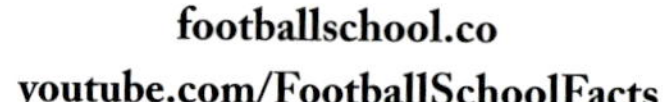
footballschool.co
youtube.com/FootballSchoolFacts

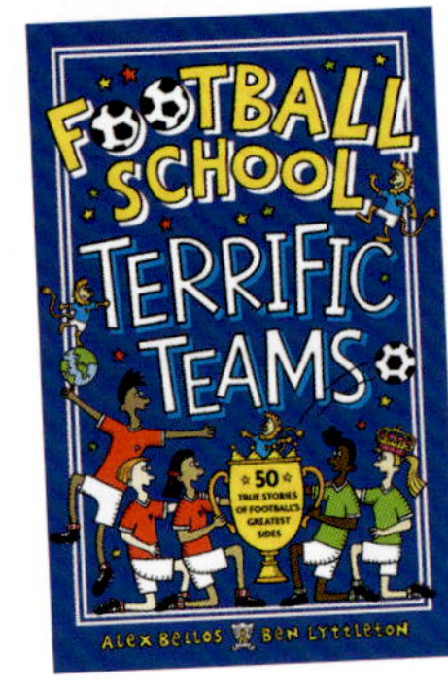
FOOTBALL SCHOOL
TERRIFIC TEAMS
50 TRUE STORIES OF FOOTBALL'S GREATEST SIDES
ALEX BELLOS BEN LYTTLETON

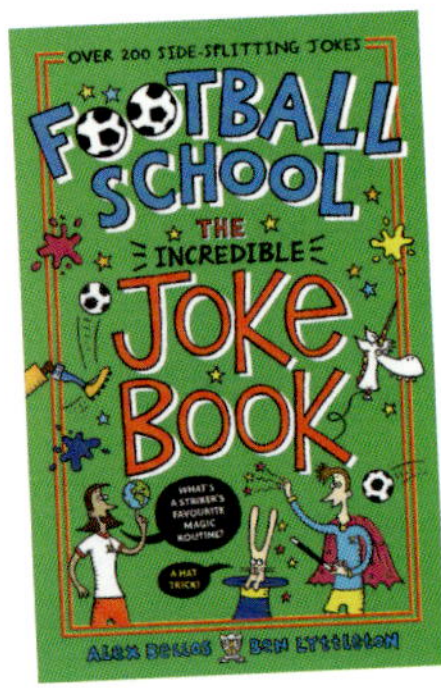
OVER 200 SIDE-SPLITTING JOKES
FOOTBALL SCHOOL
THE INCREDIBLE JOKE BOOK
ALEX BELLOS BEN LYTTLETON

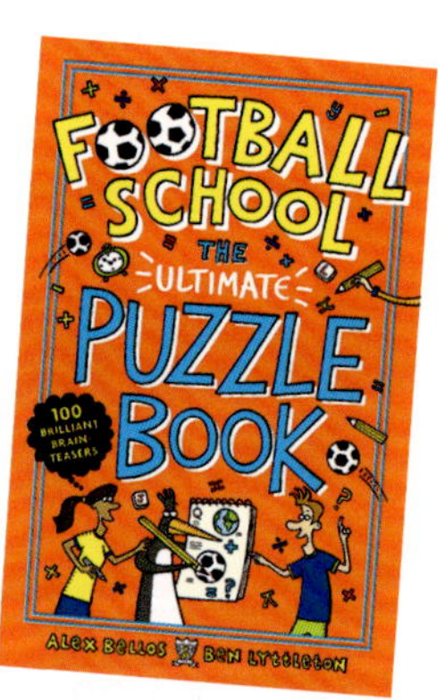
FOOTBALL SCHOOL
THE ULTIMATE PUZZLE BOOK
100 BRILLIANT BRAIN TEASERS
ALEX BELLOS BEN LYTTLETON

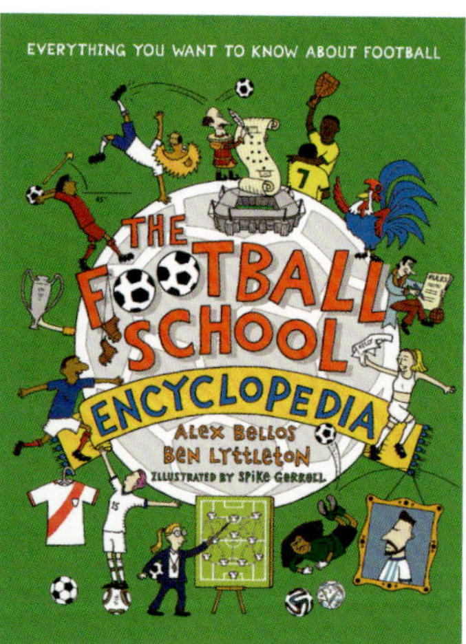
EVERYTHING YOU WANT TO KNOW ABOUT FOOTBALL
THE FOOTBALL SCHOOL ENCYCLOPEDIA
ALEX BELLOS
BEN LYTTLETON
ILLUSTRATED BY SPIKE GERRELL

OVER 300 FAN-TASTIC QUESTIONS
FOOTBALL SCHOOL
THE GREATEST EVER QUIZ BOOK
Test your football brain!
ALEX BELLOS BEN LYTTLETON